'M NOT AFRAID of the dark. But I am afraid of what may be in it. I'm afraid of what I might hear. The scratch of sharp claws against stone and then . . . a whisper.

ALSO BY JOSEPH BRUCHAC

JOSEPH BRUCHAC

WHISPER IN THE DARK

ILLUSTRATIONS BY
SALLY
WERN
COMPORT

HarperTrophy®
An Imprint of HarperCollinsPublishers

Whisper in the Dark
Copyright © 2005 by Joseph Bruchac
Illustrations copyright © 2005 by Sally Wern Comport

www.harpercollinschildrens.com

Library of Congress Cataloging-in-Publication Data
Bruchac, Joseph, 1942–
    Whisper in the dark / Joseph Bruchac ; illustrations by Sally Wern
Comport.— 1st ed.
        p. cm.
    Summary: An ancient and terrifying Narragansett native-American legend
begins to come true for a teenage long-distance runner, whose recovery from the
accident that killed her parents has stunned everyone, including her guardian
aunt in Providence, Rhode Island.
    ISBN 978-0-06-058089-6
    1. Narragansett Indians—Juvenile fiction. [1. Narragansett Indians—Fiction.
2. Indians of North America—Rhode Island—Fiction. 3. Fear—Fiction. 4. Traffic
accidents—Fiction. 5. Orphans—Fiction. 6. Aunts—Fiction. 7. Providence
(R.I.)—Fiction. 8. Rhode Island—Fiction. 9. Horror stories.] I. Comport, Sally
Wern, ill. II. Title.
PZ7.B82816Wh 2005   2004022561
[Fic]—dc22   CIP
                                                                             AC

Typography by Karin Paprocki
09 10 11 12 13 LP/CW 10 9 8 7 6 5 4 3 2 1
❖
First paperback edition, 2009

TO THE NATIVE PEOPLE OF NEW ENGLAND—
WHOSE LIVES AND STORIES
REMAIN ROOTED IN THIS LAND
—J.B.

෨ CONTENTS ෨

WHISPER
IN THE
DARK

PROLOGUE

'M WAITING HERE in the dark. It's the kind of
dark that only exists deep underground. It's so
quiet that all I can hear is my own breathing. I'm
trying to find the courage, the courage that, as my
dad told me, runs in our family.

I'm not afraid of the dark. But I am afraid of what
may be in it. I'm afraid of what I might hear. The
scratch of sharp claws against stone and then . . . a
whisper.

I usually like scary stories. But not right now.
So I've been trying not to think of any, but without
any luck. One in particular keeps forcing its way
into my mind. It's one of our old Narragansett stories, a legend from long ago. Yet as long ago as it
was told, I know now that tale is true. I've become
part of it, but I'm not sure yet what role I am going

to play, heroine or victim.

I lean back against the stone wall of the tunnel and try to regain my composure. I can't give in to fear. I try to think of something else, but all that comes into my mind is the first time I heard the tale. I'm a little girl. Grama Delia's voice is telling me how the monster came to be, that one called the Whisperer in the Dark.

It happened this way. There was a person whose mind became twisted. He was a pawwaw, one of our old-time medicine people who could speak with the manittoos, the spirits. A pawwaw is supposed to help people with his power, but this man became selfish. All that one could think of was himself, about gaining more power. So he turned to the dark manittoos. He gave them something. He gave up the daylight, and in return they gave him the power to live and keep living.

Life feeds on life. It is that way. The plant feeds on the soil and the light of the sun. The deer feeds on the plant. The wolf and the Narragansett feed on the flesh of the deer. But we must always remember the sun, look up to it and give thanks for its gift of life. If we do not do this, then we may become twisted. We may begin to believe as that one with the twisted mind believed. We may dream that we can live forever, that we never have to die.

The one with the twisted mind hid from the sun. When the clean light of the sun returned at dawn, he hid in the darkness of night and in the deep caves that go beneath our ancient hills. His fingers turned into claws and his teeth grew long. His hunger was such that he began to hunt other people, cutting their throats with his razor-sharp claws so that he could drink the blood of his victims. All that made him human left him, and he became nothing but hunger. He became a monster.

But it was not only blood that he thirsted for. He fed on the fear of his prey. Darkness grows stronger when there is fear. Few ever saw him, but our people knew that he was there. Those who were given messages in dreams knew about him. They knew that before the twisted-mind monster took its victim, the one it chose would hear a voice. A whisper. A whisper in the dark.

Only when you were his chosen victim did you hear the Whisperer's voice, that voice as hard and cold as flint. But you didn't see him, not yet. The old stories say that no one ever sees the Whisperer in the Dark when it first lets you know it's chosen you as its prey. You just hear its voice that first time. It plays with you, like a cat playing with a mouse, making you more and more terrified. It is only later, perhaps even days later, after you have become scared enough, that it will really come for you with its razor-sharp claws.

Soon, very soon, it is going to come for me.

∽ 1 ∽
WHO'S THERE?

HE FIRST CALL didn't really scare me. Not one bit. And why should it? The phone rang and I answered it.

"Hello."

Silence on the other end.

"Hello," I said again. "Hel-lo?" I was getting annoyed now. I tapped my numb left hand on the counter. A silence like that could mean that the person who called was hesitating because they had something really, really important to say. Maybe it was that reporter wanting to follow up on her article that had appeared last week about my running. It hadn't been a bad piece, despite its corny title: DESCENDANT OF CHIEFS WINS BIG MEET. Or maybe it was great news—like that I'd won a prize or something.

Or maybe something awful. Maybe this was the kind of call where the person on the other end was hesitating because they have to tell you bad news. Like someone close to you has just been hurt or even died. I knew what that kind of call was like. That kind of call makes you hold onto the phone as if it was a lifeline, the only thing to keep from falling a long, long way into a deep, deep chasm. But hard as you hold onto it, a part of you is already falling and will never stop falling. *I'm sorry* is how the person on the other end of the line begins the conversation in that sort of call. Then they say there's been an accident. And from there on in, it never gets better again.

It wasn't that kind of call. Whoever was on the other end didn't say anything, good or bad. They just hung up.

But as soon as I put the phone down and started to walk away from it, it rang again.

"Hello. Hello? HELLO?" The third time I said it, a lot louder than I'd meant to, I was starting to feel both disgusted and dumb.

But I didn't hang up. By now I just knew what it had to mean. This was one of those dumb telemarketing calls that everyone gets. Any second now I'd hear someone mispronounce Aunt Lyssa's name and then ask for a donation or try to sell us something we don't need.

But there was no sales pitch. Just more silence. The kind of silence that told me someone really was there on the other end. I couldn't hear that person breathing, but I could hear him in another way. I heard him with the sixth sense my dad's side of the family believes in so strongly. *Intuition* is what Aunt Lyssa calls it, although I think it's more than that. It's a kind of knowing. It told me there was someone on the other end of the line, listening just as intently to me. And this is when I really should have hung up. But I didn't.

Maybe it was one of my friends playing a dumb joke. Or some bored kid just dialing numbers at random for a goof.

My friend Brittany and I used to do that sort of thing on Internet chat rooms. Her persona was Ingrid, a twenty-one-year-old Swedish model. Me, I only added on five years when I identified myself as Natasha, a mysterious eighteen-year-old Gypsy ballerina from Transylvania.

I say that Brittany and I used to do that. But she and her family moved away last year, all the way out to Seattle. For a while she e-mailed me and called whenever she had a chance. But that was only for the first few months. I guess she found a new best girlfriend pretty quick. Girls like Brittany always do. I hadn't heard a word from her for months. Still, when the call came, she was the first person I thought about, so I guess I'd been missing her.

"Brittany?" I said.

The silence on the other end somehow seemed more echoey, like the silence in a cave. It was a little spooky.

"Roger?" I said. "Is that you?"

The lack of response was feeling ominous. Even if it was the middle of the morning, a sunny summer's day, it seemed as if things were getting darker around me.

I just couldn't stand it any longer. "Who's there?" I demanded.

"I am," a voice whispered. "I'm coming for you."

It was a voice as cold as ice. I felt as if spider-webs were brushing across my face. I tried to say something, but I couldn't speak.

Then the line went dead.

2
TOO SCARY

I SAT THERE STARING at the phone. I avoided touching it, as if it was a snake that might bite me. My good hand was holding my left hand so hard that my knuckles were turning white. My heart was pounding as if I'd just finished running the hundred-yard dash. I was breathing hard too. But I didn't have that satisfied feeling I get after a sprint when I've won, like I almost always do. No endorphins. No satisfied feeling. Not at all.

How could six little words hit that way, like a fist punched into my stomach? It wasn't just those words. It was the way they were spoken. It was the way they kept echoing in my mind. And I wished I had hung up sooner, that I'd never asked the question, that I had quit while there was still nothing but silence in response.

It reminded me of this one time when I was a little kid and my parents and I were in Providence visiting one of my mom's friends. She lived in an old house like Aunt Lyssa's, where I've stayed ever since I was well enough to leave the hospital and she became my legal guardian. I've finally gotten used to my aunt's place and almost think of it as my own now, even though I still have dreams that I'm back in the house in Charlestown, where I lived with my parents.

That time when I was a little kid, it was like I was in a dream, one of those dreams where you just keep walking farther and farther away from everything that is safe and real. I had drifted upstairs all alone. At the end of the hall was a dark room. I'd never been in that house before, and I had no business snooping around like that. But I couldn't help myself; I just had to go into that dark room. It was like I was being pulled in there by something, and even though I was scared out of my wits I kept taking one stupid step after another until I reached the big oak door and opened it.

You know how it is in dreams when you find yourself just having to do scary things, even though you know you shouldn't. You behave just like one of those incredibly dumb kids in scary movies. One of those nincompoops who goes off by herself into the woods to see what it was that made that sound. You know, a sound like an eight-foot-tall homicidal maniac starting his chain saw.

So there I was, in that dark room, and I didn't know where the light switch was. And just like in a dream, there was no one I knew anywhere nearby, no one who could protect me. But instead of running, I just kept walking slowly with my hands held out. And then I thought I heard a soft creak like a heavy foot and I couldn't help it. I said those two words you hear in every scary movie.

"Who's there?"

There was no answer, but my hand found a heavy curtain. I opened it and it let in just enough light to illuminate the wide-shouldered shape looming over me. That was when I screamed.

And what happened next?

Well, what do you think happened? A great big, hairy, old monster reached down and grabbed me up and ate me. I'm kidding. There was nothing more dangerous in that room than a tall old coatrack with a hat and a jacket on a coat hanger. I didn't scream for that long—maybe only ten or fifteen seconds before my mom and her friend found me and calmed me down. With the lights turned on, nothing in that room looked frightening anymore. We all ended up laughing about it.

The funny thing, though, is that it didn't cure me. I stayed just as snoopy as I had been before and just as fascinated by monsters. Like the Whisperer in the Dark. And after hearing that icy voice on the phone, all my memories of monster stories came pouring into my head.

The story of the Whisperer is a lot like the other monster stories Grama Delia shared with me. I call her Grama Delia, but she is actually the sister of my dad's grandmother. In the Narragansett way, she calls me not great-niece but granddaughter. She knows all our old Indian tales about skeletons and giants and huge birds that carry people off to eat them. Scary, but they also teach something. In our old stories, monsters only destroy those who have done lots of bad things or are so foolish that they haven't learned the lessons of survival.

Grama Delia told me other stories too. Stories

about our history and about people like the great sachem Canonchet. In 1675 the English declared war on the Narragansetts, even though most of our people didn't want to fight. Most took refuge in an island fort deep in the Great Swamp. There was a hidden trail of solid ground and stepping stones under water through a swamp that would suck down anyone who took a wrong step. Only the Narragansetts knew that hidden trail. But there was a frost the night before the English attacked. It turned the swamp into solid ground that the soldiers could cross. There was a terrible massacre. Hundreds of our people died in the Great Swamp battle. Some were men, but even more were women and children.

That wasn't the end of it, though. Instead of surrendering, Canonchet fought the English. Most of his family had died in the Great Swamp. In fact, it's been said in some history books that all his family perished there. Of course that's not true, or I wouldn't be telling you this story because my family—Grama Delia and my dad and me—are among his descendants. There aren't many of us, but we have kept the blood of Canonchet alive. He gathered the few Narragansett warriors who were left and they sought revenge. They fought a guerilla war, attacking and destroying the English towns of Warwick and Seekon and Rehobath, and then they came to Providence.

"Right back there by the Providence River," Grama Delia told me, "is where Roger Williams came walking out to ask them to spare his town. But Canonchet shook his head. 'I am sorry, friend Roger,' Canonchet said. 'Your town too must be destroyed.' But he allowed Roger Williams and his people safe passage out before they burned nearly all of the houses that made up Providence then."

A few weeks later, in April, Canonchet was taken captive by the Mohegan allies of the English. His last words were "I like it well. I shall die before my heart is soft or before I have said anything unworthy of myself." Then they killed him.

Grama Delia told me how, after the death of our great ancestor Canonchet, the war ended. Our people had been broken, and many of those who survived were sold into slavery or ended up as indentured servants to the English. But they remembered the stories of their people and the history of all that happened to them. They passed it down, not in books but through storytelling.

Our Narragansett stories take me way back to the old times. Those stories have been here a lot longer than the houses and cars and streets that most everyone takes for granted here in Providence. Most people today haven't learned what some of their own old houses know. Houses have memories that go even deeper than their walls. Old houses are connected to the earth that was there before they were built. They see with their windows, just like we do with our eyes. Some people, like Grama Delia, can actually look at the windows of certain old houses and see scenes from the past reflected in them. Just like watching a TV screen.

That is what Grama Delia's stories have always been like for me. Through the windows of her stories, I could see what was here—and still is here. I could really see the glowing eyes of the cannibal skeleton or the long-nosed, heavy-bodied walking hill when she told me about them.

I usually loved it when she told me our old tales. The scarier the better. They reminded me that even little kids can defeat a monster if they know the right thing to do. No story was ever too scary for me—until she started to tell me about the Whisperer in the Dark.

The night when she began the story, I had insisted that since I was now all of nine years old, I was ready to hear her very scariest tale. Even then I had this fascination for anything about the supernatural, and I was sure I could handle it. But I'd been wrong. I soon started crying, and Mom put her arms around me. That made me feel better, but Grama Delia figured I'd had enough. She tied a knot in the tale.

"There is more to the story," Grama Delia said. "But it can wait until later. Just remember, little one, nothing that hides in the dark is ever stronger than the sun. Now it's time for your mother to tuck you in your bed."

The Whisperer in the Dark? Why was I suddenly thinking about that now? What was wrong with me? All that had happened was that I got a couple of dumb prank phone calls. I was blowing this way out of proportion. Instead of feeling afraid, I started feeling angry. I wasn't some dumb kid in a movie or one of those heroines who had to wait for a prince to save her. Indian girls in our stories always knew how to take care of themselves.

Then I remembered. Nowadays if you get an anonymous call, all you have to do is dial * 69. It'll give you the number of your last incoming call so that you can ring back and tell them you know who they are and they had better stop bothering you or you will call the police.

With a superior smile on my face, I reached for the phone. Be logical, calm. Dial *69. That was what I was going to do. But before I could touch it, the phone rang again. And in spite of myself, I screamed.

❦ 3 ❦

TOO MUCH IMAGINATION

I JUST STARED AT the ringing phone. I wasn't really freaked out. I didn't pick it up. I didn't have to. I could do something else. I had choices, lots of choices. I could rip the phone off the wall and hurl the darn thing out the window. Or I could run up to my bedroom like some demented nitwit and bury my head under a pillow.

Or I could sprint out into the street screaming for help—as if that would do any good. At this time of day in July, nobody is ever home in this neighborhood. They're either at work or off to the beach or something. Like I would have been if I hadn't had this weird midsummer cold that made me feel so achy and tired that Aunt Lyssa told me to just go ahead and sleep in.

It wasn't like I'd been hypnotized by that whispery

voice or frozen with fear like the people in that creepy story Grama Delia told about the Whisperer. Or was I?

This was stupid. I was just scaring myself. Maybe psycho killers in films call people, but not old-time monsters from Narragansett stories. No way. Totally ridiculous. Imagine the Whisperer in the Dark calling the telephone company to have them hook him up with a plan. Imagine a monster that no one has ever seen and lived to talk about listening to some sales rep at a mall babble on about what kind of service he wants on his cell phone.

Come on, Maddy, I thought to myself. *Get real. It was just six little words.*

Too much of an imagination. That was why I'd let that dumb phone call get to me. People were probably right when they said I'd read too many books about morbid stuff. Mr. Mindlow, the school psychologist, thinks I'm fascinated by "horror media" because I lost my parents, and thus scary stories and monster movies are safe and even reassuring for me because they are not real. That is why, he says, I am always reading Anne Rice or Providence's own favorite haunted son, nutty old

H. P. Lovecraft himself. That is why all my favorite rentals are in the science fiction/horror/suspense section of MovieLand. And I have the world's biggest collection of *Fangoria* magazine. Because all the blood and fear and mortality is under my control.

Even though I'm not as tragically out of balance as Mr. Mindlow thinks, I suppose he is sort of right. You can always walk out of a movie or turn off a TV, even in the middle of the most awful events. You know that, after the filming is over, all the people who get "killed" are really still alive, and the monsters are all fake. I've seen loads of documentaries on makeup and special effects. It's comforting to see the same character actors getting glommed up by evil beings in one movie after another. It is like they are immortal. Even death is imaginary.

But the phone on the wall was not imaginary. Nor was that voice. It was too real.

The phone rang again. And I finally did something. I grabbed it and yelled "What do you want?"

"I vant your blood," said a voice with a thick accent.

~ 4 ~
SCRATCHING

I F THE PERSON saying those words with that phony accent had been close enough, I would have grabbed him and shoved one of his Anne Rice novels down his throat.

"Grow up," I growled.

"Blagh! Vot is the matter, pathetic mortal?"

"Roger Tillinghast, you are an idiot! Just stop it!" Maybe it was because my own voice trembled as I said this that his immediately changed.

"Aw, Maddy, ah'm sorry. What's wrong?"

No more phony Count Dracula, just his usual New Orleans drawl. Roger's name and roots are just as Rogue Island as mine. His family goes back about as far as anyone who isn't Narragansett. But Roger's dad and mom were living in Louisiana when he was born. They only moved back to his grandmother's house on Federal Hill when his mom got hired by the English department at Brown. Her family is from Cranston, which is part of greater Providence. Her specialty is the Gothic tradition in novels, so she is right at home here in more ways than one.

"Did you just call me?" I said.

"You mean right now?"

"No, before this, like a minute ago."

"No, ma'am."

"Are you sure?"

"Honest Injun."

I groaned a little at that, which had been his intention. We were good enough friends to tease each other that way, like my saying "That was white of you," sort of semi-sarcastically whenever he did something dumb. It's the kind of thing real friends can do with each other. And I knew right then that I really needed to have a friend around.

"Can you come over?" I said. "Now."

"Okay," Roger said. "In a flash."

He didn't ask why or demand to be told what was up. Even though we'd only known each other for less than a year, he'd already learned what most of my other friends didn't understand. Don't ask

Maddy Brown what is going on when she's acting upset. When she's being Moody Maddy. But he did ask one thing before he hung up.

"Ten K?"

"At least," I answered, looking out the window. It was cloudy, but it looked like the rain would hold off for a while. It was almost time for the weather on the local news, so I turned on the TV. Sure enough, after one of their daytime anchors finished her story about the university archaeological team continuing excavations on a cave site close to Providence, Red the Better Weatherman popped up on the screen, pointer in hand. Expect scattered showers all afternoon. Just what we need for those summer gardens.

As soon as I hung up, I got my gear together. Roger didn't live that far away. He would soon be at my door. Thinking of us running together was making me feel normal again.

I love running with Roger right by my side, keeping step with me no matter how fast I go. Even though his legs are longer than mine, he has a relatively short stride, and we run together like a matched team of horses. I noticed that ten months ago when we were warming up at the same time on the school track. That was the real start of my friendship with the new guy whose cute Southern accent and shy ways had made him a target for half the girls in my class. Except he chose me.

I'd really needed somebody like Roger then. Not as a boyfriend, just somebody I could trust—and it was an added bonus that he loved to run like I did. I still couldn't talk then about the accident that took the lives of my parents. Just mentioning it made me feel as if I was back in the car with them on that March evening when a freak ice storm blew in from the north. Mom had been driving, but none of us saw the black ice on the hill before we hit it. I don't think it would have been any different if Dad had been behind the wheel. He'd always said that Mom was a safer driver than he was. Neither of them panicked.

"Make sure your seat belt is fastened," my mom said to me without looking back, both her hands still on the wheel.

"You're doing fine, honey," Dad said to her. His hand was on her shoulder. They were so together at that moment, and I remember realizing then how much they loved each other. And then the tree came through the windshield.

There were, I know, lots of rumors about me at school. Rumors about why I have this one dead hand. (Nerve damage from getting my hand crushed in the wreck. The doctors say it might heal itself or never get any better.) Rumors that my whole body is covered with terrible scars. (It isn't.) Rumors about my being an orphan because of some kind of tragedy. (You know about that.)

Sometimes people even ask me. Like that reporter who wrote the story about an Indian girl, one of the last descendants of Canonchet, winning the interstate cross-country meet. But I never answered questions about the rumors. I just changed the subject or didn't say anything.

I was afraid that was what Roger was going to do that day on the track. Ask me about my hand or my scars or my mom and dad.

"Hey," he said, looking over at me as he stretched his quads.

I braced myself, waiting for the question. But he didn't ask it.

"I was watching you run yesterday. Want to

run with me?" he asked.

"Okay," I said.

By the end of that week, I'd discovered that talking with Roger was as easy as running with him.

When I found out he was as nutty about horror stuff as I was, that his mom even taught Gothic fiction, I felt like jumping in the air to give anyone close enough to me a high five. Sweet. Best of all, Roger didn't mind listening to me; in fact, he even seemed to like to hear me talk. And he didn't make things all boy-girl complicated like a lot of other guys would. Even though I'm self-conscious about the fact that my left hand is like a carved piece of wood, Aunt Lyssa says that is not the first thing people notice about me. What they see, she says, are my eyes and the shape of my face. My mom looked a lot like I do, but the blend of Dad's Indian blood with her Sicilian fire (as Aunt Lyssa puts it) makes me look like an exotic model. That gives some guys the wrong idea until I set them straight. But not Roger. He's always seen me as a regular person, and that's why I can see him as a friend, my very best friend.

While I pulled on my running clothes and my

sneakers, I didn't do what some people do when they've been scared. I didn't try to focus my mind on bunny rabbits or kitty cats or Disney cartoons (which, quite frankly, I find to be *truly* scary). Instead I mentally ran through the whole catalog of scary creatures from Narragansett tales: Cheepi, the Evil One; huge black dogs; headless ghosts; cannibal skeletons; underwater snakes; monster birds. We even have a story about the devil on ice skates. I thought about all those different creatures that Grama Delia made come alive for me in her wintertime tales, so alive that I only had to close my eyes to see them. And especially I thought about how each and every one of them ended up defeated or thwarted in one way or another.

Like I said, monsters are one of the reasons Roger and I became so close so quick. They are his favorite thing too. We both like them because the best monster stories—not just the ones that Grama Delia told me about, but even some of the newer ones in books and movies—always have rules and a certain kind of supernatural logic to them. First there's the battle between good and evil, then there's the idea that good can always find some way to win. That's usually linked to the fact that, powerful as any monster might be, it always has at least one weakness. That was even true of those scary creations of poor old neurotic HPL, the "ghoul-haunted master of the macabre" (as Roger's mother calls him). A kid can take comfort in that, knowing that even a little child can find a way to overcome a big old monster. "The reassurance of juvenile empowerment." That's how Roger's mother explains it in her lectures.

A rumbling sound came from down the road. A construction crew had been there for the last two weeks, doing some kind of excavating for a new sewer line or something. Aunt Lyssa had been told that they'd only have the street torn up for a few days. That had made both of us smile. Nothing in Providence ever gets done in a few days. Apparently they'd run into harder rock than expected because they were now using dynamite. That was unfortunate. Every time a blast went off—like the one that had just made me drop my running shoes—it totally freaked out Bootsie to the point where she peed on the rug. As a result, she had been banished during the day to our fenced-in backyard. Bootsie is a year-old Irish setter. Aunt Lyssa got her as a puppy because she said I needed a dog to keep me company. Of course, Aunt Lyssa is the one "my" dog always comes to first. And guess whose bed she sleeps on at night?

I heard her scratching on the back door as I started putting on my shoes, once again thanking the gods of new technologies for Velcro straps.

"Bootsie, cut it out," I yelled. "Aunt Lyssa is going to kill you if you mark up that new paint."

When the doorbell rang, I congratulated myself on not jumping at the sudden sound. Still, I did look through the side window before I opened the front door.

"Hey, Rog," I said. Everything was cool now. No problema.

"Yo, Mad," he said. There was a question in his eyes, but he didn't ask it. "Ready to sweat?" he asked instead.

I started to say yes, but then I remembered the dog.

"Wait, gotta let Bootsie in. Darn dog always has to come in through the back door."

Roger walked with me as I tromped through the

house and threw the door open.

"Boots?" I said.

But she wasn't there.

Roger tapped me on the shoulder.

"Maddy," he said, pointing at something. "Man oh man? What the heck is that?"

I looked at the newly painted back door. The back of my neck tingled as I read the three words scratched deeply into the wood:

I AM HERE

5
SCARY CITY

WHAT'S THIS ABOUT, Mad?" Roger's fingers reached out to touch the letters, which could only have been been scored so deeply by a very sharp blade—or a claw. There was a little smile on his face. I knew it was because he was getting a thrill from the creepiness of the situation.

It was the same smile Roger had on his face when I had taken him on my own special Running and Eating Horror Tour of Providence after finding out that not only was he an ace Cross-country Crazy, he was also a nut for supernatural stuff.

The two of us set out that day from Waterplace Park. We did the whole Banner Trail, up and down Smithy Hill, back and forth across the bridges, sprinting and sightseeing, taking in not just the museums and the urban architecture, but also those special places sacred to scarydom. East Side, West Side, College Hill always in sight.

I can still see him holding a Dell's Lemonade in one hand while reaching out with the other to lightly caress the door frame of the Atheneum.

"Man oh man! Edgar Allan Poe touched this here, ah'll bet," he said in a soft voice as he stared through the door of the old library.

As Roger ate his third Al's New York System weiner, proving once again that all Cross-country runners are bottomless pits, I introduced him to a certain gabled New England colonial on Benefit Street. "The Shunned House" was the abode of a buried vampire in HPL's creepy yarn. Then, after devouring one of Newport Creameries' Awful Awful Sundaes, I pointed out the steeple of that church on Federal Hill where a dreaded winged monster perched in yet another of the Master's hair-raising tales.

After running Blackstone Boulevard, we jogged and then slowed to a stroll to enter Swan Point Cemetery, where the cliffs look out over the Seekonk River, toward where the excavations were just starting into a recently discovered cave in the steepest part of the cliff face. I'd read about it in the papers and knew that it was sponsored by some wealthy guy who was convinced that the ancient Chinese had landed here a century before Columbus. Our Narragansett Tribal Council had been concerned that the cave might contain some ancestral graves. But the people in charge had assured them that they were certain the cave wasn't the site of any Indian burials. As if we'd never heard that before. Any time archaeologists start digging up the ground here in New England, they usually come across Indian burial sites. Over the last few years, our people had managed to put a stop to much of this. My dad had been very involved. We'd also been able to get back a lot of the bones of our ancestors from museums and colleges so they could be decently reburied.

Roger and I walked past the graves of Rhode Island Volunteers who gave their lives in the Civil War.

And then we came at last to *the* grave. Howard Phillips Lovecraft's last resting place. H. P. Lovecraft, author of some of the most chilling Gothic tales of ancient evil ever written. 1890–1937. Roger went down on one knee, and his long fingers traced the letters on the stone.

"'I am Providence,'" he read aloud—with no trace at all of that weird New Orleans accent that sounds like you put a street kid from Brooklyn into a bottle with a Georgia Cracker and then shook it. And then that smile came over his face.

The same smile was on Roger's face now as he looked at the words "I am here" on my door.

For just a moment, I wondered if this *was* all just a joke and if Roger really did do it. Was it possible that he was the one who called me the first two times, even though he said he didn't? Was it his hand that scratched the words into the back door? As soon as I asked myself those questions, I shook my head. Even though he loves weird stuff to death, Roger is my friend and wouldn't try to really freak me out. He isn't a mean practical joker. He was probably smiling because he thought I'd set this up to show him that the supernatural was still alive and well in Rogue Island.

And there is no way that he could have gotten around front to knock on the door only a heartbeat

after I heard the scratching stop. The back gate was still closed and locked from the inside. The high fence was around my backyard. It was meant to keep in Bootsie, who like all year-old Irish setters would have been running her fool head off halfway across town, following her goofy nose, without that barrier.

Where was Bootsie? Why hadn't she barked when the doorbell rang? She always barked like crazy whenever she heard or saw anyone. And if something scared her—like the crack of thunder or the sudden ground-shaking rumble from the blasting going on a couple of blocks away from us—as soon as anyone opened the door she was in the house like a shot, woofing and whining and trying to crawl under my bed. Why wasn't she making a sound now, and where the heck was she? The only reason a hyperactive dog like Bootsie would be quiet would be because she was asleep or . . .

"Bootsie," I called, looking wildly around the yard. "Bootsie? BOOTSIE!"

6

BLOOD

ROGER AND I searched the backyard. We checked the back gate. It was still locked. There was no way Bootsie could have gotten out. Maybe a really athletic person—or something that had the kind of claws that allowed it to climb chain link—could have gotten over it, but not a dog like Boots. The kind of fence Aunt Lyssa had put in was meant to be dog-proof. It was even buried two feet deep so Bootsie couldn't dig under it.

We both started whistling and calling her name.

"Boots, here, girl. Come on, Bootsie."

But she didn't come. The sick feeling in my stomach got worse and worse.

"Mad," Roger said in an urgent voice. I turned. He was on his knees, looking under the shed. "There's something here. Got a torch?"

I grabbed the big flashlight Aunt Lyssa kept in the kitchen cupboard and sprinted back to where Roger was squinting into the darkness of the crawl-space below the shed. The first thing my flashlight beam picked up was a dark, wet spot in the dirt. I touched it and then looked at the red stain on my finger.

"Oh no," I said, "it's blood."

Roger nudged my shoulder. "Back farther, Mad, way back under there. I think I see something else."

I was really dreading what I'd see, but I directed the bright shaft of light back to the farthest corner under the shed. There was a huddled shape with a matted red coat. Bootsie. I felt numb. I just knew that she was dead. I handed the flashlight to Roger.

"I'm going after her," I said. "Hold the light so I can see."

Roger didn't try to protest. He knew how I was when I set my mind to something. That was why I went back to running two months after the accident, even though the doctors had said it'd be a year before I could exercise again. They doubted I'd even be much of a runner again with one hand so messed up. But I set my mind to it and proved them wrong, winning my first ten K before the end of that year.

I squeezed myself farther under the shed. The space was so low that I scraped my back as I crawled forward on my elbows. It was only a dozen feet, but it seemed to take forever. At last I could reach my good right hand out far enough. When it touched Bootsie's back, my heart leaped. Her skin was warm.

She trembled at my touch and whimpered. It was the same sound she used to make when she was a tiny puppy hiding from the rumble of thunder. I got hold of her collar and began to inch back, trying to drag her limp, unresisting body with me. Roger grabbed my ankles and pulled. Between the two of us, we managed to get her out into the sunlight.

As soon as Bootsie felt the light, it was if her On button had been pushed. She scrambled to her feet and started to bark. She licked my face and Roger's hands, jumping around us in the kind of glad hysteria that Irish setters go into when they've been alone a really long time—like say five minutes. Roger helped me calm her down.

"Mad," he said, getting down on his knees, "check this out." He gently lifted her right front paw. As he did so, Bootsie whined and made a little chewing motion toward his hand, but she didn't bite.

"Here's where the blood came from, Mad," Roger said. "Once a dog gets a cut on its pad, it just bleeds like a stuck pig. Probably caught it on a loose nail."

The cut was clean, as clean as if it had been made with a razor. But it didn't explain her fear. There had to be something more. I slid my right hand carefully along Bootsie's body. She began to tremble as I got close to her right hip, where the fur was matted and dark. She went down onto her side and tried to roll away, but Roger kept a firm grip on her collar.

"Look here," I whispered.

Roger let out a soft whistle. There on Bootsie's flank were four more slash wounds. No loose nail made them. It was if they were made by a handful of knives—or by four razor-sharp claws.

7

THE DEEP END

MY FINGERS WERE turning red from the blood welling out of the deep cuts on Bootsie's flank. Everything around me began to slow down. I knew that Bootsie was still whimpering, but I could no longer hear her. I wanted to say something, but I couldn't breathe.

When I was six years old, I fell into the deep end of the swimming pool at the park and sank to the cool bottom. I didn't think to try to use my arms or legs to save myself. My eyes were open, and I could see the blurry shapes of other people swimming, their legs kicking above me. None of them seemed to know I was there. I could no longer hear voices, and there was just a soft roaring in my ears. It wasn't scary. It was kind of calm at the cold bottom of the pool, peaceful. Then, just as I couldn't hold my breath any longer and was about to close my eyes, someone grabbed me from behind and pulled me up to the surface. There was a rush of water, then the cold touch of the air and people shouting and shaking me.

Shaking me. The way Roger was shaking me, making me breathe. A trembling breath that was almost a sob.

"What should we do, Mad?" Roger was saying.

I looked up at him. Roger is tall for his age, taller than a lot of grown men. He's really strong and his shoulders are broad, much broader than the usual kid who's a good long-distance runner. That's why the high school football coaches kept trying to get him to come out for the team. But Roger was determined to be a runner, even if he wasn't built right for it. And he succeeded. That determination of his kept him going when others would quit in that last uphill half mile before the line. Determined as he was, though, Roger was looking at me, expecting me to tell him what to do. I reached into the shed and pulled out an old, clean beach towel.

"Take this," I said to Roger. "I'll lift her up a little, and you can wrap it around her like a bandage.

We've got to get her to Dr. Fox."

Then I ran back inside and grabbed my backpack and cell phone. As I walked around the house closing it up, I used the phone to first call for a taxi. Then I tried Aunt Lyssa's office. As I expected, I just got her machine. Everything that was happening was too complicated and confusing to explain in the twenty seconds I had to leave her a message, so I just said that Bootsie got hurt, but she'd probably be all right, and that Roger and I were taking her to our vet. I made sure the windows were latched—upstairs and down. I locked all the doors, not just the front and back, but also the big heavy one that leads down to our old stone-walled, earth-floor cellar. But I was still feeling nervous.

I felt a little better when the taxi driver arrived. He'd been to my house before, and he knew us. His name was Raj Patel, and he was from India. He was a nice man with a shy, friendly smile and a gentle voice. He didn't object one bit when Roger climbed in with Bootsie, even though it was clear from the red stain on the towel that she was still bleeding. He just shook his head and said, "We must hurry her to the veterinarian."

It was only a couple of miles to our vet's clinic, but it was long enough for me to reach his receptionist on the cell phone and tell her we were coming in with Bootsie and it was an emergency. It also took us longer than usual because we had to take a detour just before the TURN OFF RADIOS BLASTING IN PROGRESS sign. As a result, good old Doc Fox was waiting outside when we pulled into his driveway, looking like a big, unkempt bear that had somehow been thrust into a neat white surgeon's coat.

"Here," Doc Fox rumbled, thrusting out his huge arms to take Bootsie and whisking her back into the clinic.

I tried to pay Mr. Patel, but he waved his hand at me.

"It is all right," he said. "You are a regular customer."

"Thank you," I said. I was feeling emotional, and his kindness touched me so much that it was hard not to start crying.

Mr. Patel smiled. "Don't mention it. I am just glad to see that your dog was not killed like all the other ones."

"All *what* other ones?" Even though it was a warm day, I felt a chill, like cold water trickling down my back.

Mr. Patel shook his head. "Have you not heard? There have been several dogs killed, just near where you are living. Some fierce animal, it appears, attacked them. Most strange, indeed."

I could hardly feel my feet touching the sidewalk. I was back in the deep end of the pool.

8
WAITING

ROGER AND I sat and waited. I thought of how concerned Doc Fox had looked. By the time we got there, Bootsie had gotten much weaker. She'd barely been able to lift her head to lick his shoulder.

"Good girl," he'd growled. Doc Fox never talks much, and when he does it's in half sentences. I also don't know if anyone has ever heard him use the personal pronoun for himself.

"Take a seat," he'd rumbled, motioning toward his waiting room with his chin. Then he and Bootsie had vanished into the back.

And after that, time, which had been speeding along like a runaway train, slowed to a crawl. The hands on Doc Fox's old-fashioned clock seemed welded in place. I tried counting under my breath.

One and one thousand, two and one thousand.

I made half an hour pass that way. We were still waiting. I was as fidgety as a squirrel trapped in a cage, but Roger just sat there, calm, his hands in his lap. I like that relaxed quality of his. He almost always seems at ease, comfortable with himself. He isn't one of those annoying people who talks just to make noise or flails his arms around to get attention. He generally does just what's right for the occasion. Just then he knew all he could do was wait, so that was what he was doing. He wasn't even reading one of the tattered old *National Geographic* magazines that were stacked like a messy yellow mountain on the wicker table in the waiting room.

Me, I was rapidly becoming one of those annoying people. I kept standing up, sitting down, looking at the door, at the desk, out the window. I flipped through the one copy of *People* magazine that had infiltrated the table with those *National Geographic*s like a rock star who accidentally stumbled into a retirement party. Famous people, pretty clothes, new houses, hot cars. I tried to read it, but it made me think of movie popcorn, overpriced and mostly air. Nothing could take my

mind off Bootsie or what had been happening . . .
or what might happen next.

"Roger," I said.

"Uh-huh," he answered, putting his hand on my
shoulder.

Then neither of us said anything more. I had a
friend close by right now. That made me feel a little
less scared.

I thought of calling Aunt Lyssa. Maybe I would
hear her real voice this time—not just that recorded
message telling me to speak at the sound of the
tone. It was almost time for her to be back from her
lunch break at the library. I thought, too, of calling
Grama Delia. If anyone would understand what was
happening, she would. Even though some folks
think she's full of superstitions and old beliefs that
mean nothing, I've always known different.

The last time I was there a bird had flown in
through the open window of her little house. It was
a small brown flycatcher. It had darted around,
fluttering its wings and chirping. But it hadn't
seemed frantic and it didn't touch anything before
it flew out again. Grama Delia and I had looked at
each other.

We had both smiled. She didn't even have to tell me that we had just experienced a good omen.

A good omen. I looked back up at the clock. Only one more minute had passed. I needed a good omen now as I sat in the waiting room. But I didn't call Grama Delia. I couldn't make my fingers press the numbers. I just couldn't call anyone until I found out how Bootsie was.

At least three full years went by before Doc Fox came out into the waiting room, even though the clock on the wall tried to pretend it had only been forty-five minutes. He was shaking his head.

I stood up, so quickly it made me feel a little dizzy. I just knew he was going to tell me that my Bootsie was dead. It would be just like it was when I was in the hospital and I woke up and they told me. . . .

But Doc Fox thrust out his hand, motioning for me to sit down, be calm. "She's okay," he said. "She'll be fine. I'll keep her here overnight." Then he held out both his big paws, palms up.

"Madeline," he asked, "what?"

I knew what he meant by that single word. What happened to Bootsie? What did that to her?

I shook my head. He nodded his head back at me and growled under his breath. It was like we were two bears, communicating like bears do when they move their heads back and forth to show they are feeling amicable.

"I worked awhile," he said, "at a zoo. Two tigers had a fight. Had to sedate 'em, stitch them up." He paused and looked up at one of his degrees on the wall, as if some kind of answer was written there.

I nodded, getting this creepy feeling that I knew where he was going with this.

"Thing is," he said, "Bootsie's wounds are like that. Wide, deep, like tiger claws."

9

SOMETHING WORSE

A S ROGER AND I walked down the hill toward the center of Old Providence, I wasn't really sure where I was heading. I'd thought of walking home or maybe down to Aunt Lyssa's library. There was nothing more we could do at the clinic. Doc Fox had said that he needed to keep Bootsie there overnight and so we might as well go home.

As for what it was that had attacked her, Doc Fox had finally suggested that perhaps someone had a big pet cat, maybe a cougar, that either escaped or was just let go by someone who got tired of caring for it. It had to be some private owner because he'd put in a call to the Roger Williams Park and learned that no dangerous creatures had escaped from there lately—or ever, for that matter. It was illegal, he'd explained, for a private citizen to own such dangerous predators, but that kind of law has never stopped people who are wealthy and insensitive enough. There's a big trade smuggling exotic animals and endangered species into this country. South American mountain lions, ocelots, African leopards.

"Strange, though," he had added, "that this mystery cat wasn't declawed."

By that he'd meant that most people who purchased a huge feline predator as an illicit pet had the animal's claws removed when it was little—and not just to save their furniture. You know how it is when your pet kitty cat gets cranky and takes a swipe at you? Imagine a mountain lion doing that! What it meant for the animal was that a life in captivity was its only option for survival. Just last year there'd been a story on TV about a hunter in Maine shooting an animal that turned out to be one of those declawed captive mountain lions someone had let go. The poor creature had been nothing but skin and bones.

Doc Fox had said he'd be letting the police know that there seemed to be a cougar or leopard or something of that sort on the loose. My intuition, though, wasn't accepting that. I didn't know what the real answer was, but I just felt that it was something worse. That's one problem with intuition. Sometimes it's as if you're hearing someone tell you something really important—but they're speaking in a language you can't understand.

We were strolling along, but my thoughts were running. I'd tried calling Aunt Lyssa again. No luck. Still just the recording. I'd also decided not to go back to the house. The thought of what had happened there was creeping me out. First the phone calls, then the scratching on the door, and then Bootsie. Just thinking of it made me feel like screaming. Instead I was babbling on about something I'd just seen in that issue of *People* magazine.

"Did you see that picture of her dress? How can anyone live that way. And what kind of car was that?"

Roger just nodded. There was no way to reply to the kind of wacky monologue I was delivering. Even I wasn't sure what I was talking about. It was like my mouth was on autopilot while my brain was in a crash dive. I felt as if I needed to run away, find a safe place to hide, but instead I kept walking. We could have headed toward the library, to find Aunt Lyssa, but when we came to the turn, I went the other way. Aunt Lyssa is always so upbeat about everything that at times it drives me crazy. Like just the other day when I was complaining about how greenhouse gasses were causing global warming, she replied that it might be nice to have warmer summers and shorter winters. I wasn't ready to see her yet, to be reassured that everything was all right. I just needed to talk and keep walking. And that was what I did, thankful that I had Roger there.

Roger is so great. Like the good friend he is, he was sticking by me and not asking questions. He knew, despite the fact that I was talking and laughing like some TV valley girl, that I was anything but carefree right now.

I'd said all that could possibly be said about that issue of the magazine. So now I started talking about the weather, about the summer cross-country meets that were coming up, about stopping off at the next New York System weiner stand because I was feeling starved. But when we did come to that hot dog stand, I couldn't stop. I was trying to keep my voice calm and light, but I could feel it getting higher in pitch and almost hysterical.

I think people were turning to look at me as we went down Benefit Street. I'm usually quiet on that street. I really appreciate all those old restored buildings and like to look around at them. If you're a nut for brick sidewalks and cobblestone alleys, mansard roofs, gables, and wrought-iron railings, Benefit Street is like heaven for you. But I might as well have been walking through the mall for all the attention I paid to the architecture this time. I didn't even point out the Governor Hopkins House where George Washington slept. Twice.

Finally we reached Market House down by the river, which is always busy. It was the first marketplace of Old Providence. Before that it was the crossroads where the trails met that led from the Pequots in Connecticut and the Wampanoags in Massachusetts. Even before the coming of foreign sailors from across the sea, this had been a meeting place of different nations, each with their own ways and their own histories to tell.

Here, close to the water of the Providence River, with lots of people around, with all that remembered history surrounding me, I felt better. That is kind of a strange thing to say, I suppose, considering how much of that history is painful to remember if you are an Indian. After all, the coming of the Europeans brought warfare and diseases and laws that took away first our land and then even our tribal status, like in 1880 when the Rhode Island legislature declared our whole tribe extinct. Thinking about it, feeling the melancholy pain of being Indian that Dad and I used to talk about, made me calmer, because it was so familiar. Because I'd felt that way a thousand times before while standing here looking out at our river that leads down into Narragansett Bay.

"Roger," I said.

"Uh-huh," he answered.

But before I could say anything, my cell phone rang. It was so unexpected, so much a part of the modern world and not where my gloomy thoughts of doom had been taking me, that it made me laugh.

"It's for you," Roger said. It was a dumb thing to say, but the way he said it was so funny that it made me laugh even harder. Somehow I managed to get the phone out. But before answering it, I looked at the Caller ID and then sighed with relief. I knew that number.

"Aunt Lyssa," I said into the phone.

"Honey." Just that single word in my aunt's gentle voice made me feel better. "Maddy, honey, I got your message about Bootsie. Is she all right?"

"Bootsie's going to be okay. Doc Fox is keeping her overnight," I said. "Roger's here with me."

"That's good," Aunt Lyssa said. "You want to bring him home? I'm picking up chicken for dinner."

I sighed with relief. This was all so normal. I looked over at Roger, who had been leaning close enough to hear my aunt's side of our conversation. He nodded his head.

"Okay," I said.

"We'll talk when I get home," Aunt Lyssa said in her positive way. "Everything is going to be all right."

I felt that way when I put my phone away. Everything was fine. There was nothing to worry about. But as Roger and I walked back up Benefit Street, that good feeling seeped away. And Aunt Lyssa's reassuring voice was replaced by another one, a voice that whispered fear.

10

WHO IS THAT?

I FLUFFED UP MY pillow for the twentieth time. I was exhausted, but I couldn't sleep. We'd eaten dinner with Aunt Lyssa, and then Roger and I had played my new video game which is loosely based on a movie that is loosely based on a character out of Bram Stoker's *Dracula*. We'd gotten bored fast. It was all monsters and explosions and was way over the top. The really scary stuff isn't like *Star Wars* with werewolves and vampires who look like the Incredible Hulk with fangs and claws. Real horror creeps up on you.

We ended up turning off the PlayStation and just talking about normal stuff like other kids at school and our teachers and running. We'd talked a lot about Bootsie at dinner, how weird it was the way she was hurt. We were no longer worried about

how she was recovering. Dr. Fox had left a message that she was doing great. He was just keeping her for a day or two to make sure she didn't have an infection or something. Aunt Lyssa acted like everything was all cool, but she must have known I was still freaked out about Bootsie because she was the one who suggested calling Roger's parents to see if he could sleep over in the spare bedroom. I wondered if he was sleeping now. I sure wasn't. My mind kept going back, not just to Bootsie getting hurt but to those phone calls. None of it made sense.

Think about something else, I told myself. So I tried focusing on how safe and secure I was here in my bed, here in my room in this house that had become my home.

Then I began thinking about this house, about how old it is, from its gabled roof on down to its fieldstone foundation. That made me think about the cellar. It's a real cellar, not one of those neatly sealed basements that can be turned into a rec room or a den with windows that open to the outside like you see in modern houses. Our cellar was dug into the ground, into the old stones of the hills of Providence. It's always cool and even a little damp in the cellar, and although it lacks windows, it does have doors, three of them.

Those doors are the first things you see when you come down the creaky wooden stairs. The door to the right of the stairs leads to a small, square root cellar, just about the size of one of the prison cells in *The Count of Monte Cristo*. The door in front opens to the furnace room and the storage bin where the coal used to be shoveled in from outside. The door to the left is the one that is never opened.

That third cellar door is made of thick wood, heavy oak with huge metal hinges. I don't know why it's so thick and heavy, strong enough to hold against almost anything that might try to break it down. Maybe it's just because that was the way some doors were built three centuries ago. A lot stronger than the new door at the top of the creaky cellar stairs.

Had I locked that new door down into the cellar? For some reason the thought of it being unlocked made me feel panicked. No, I'd locked it. I'd done that first, even before latching the windows when we'd taken Bootsie to the vet.

When I was little and just visiting Aunt Lyssa,

not actually living in the house, I would scare myself by thinking about how that third door in the cellar used to lead into the tunnels. It was kept locked to keep people from going in and getting lost or maybe buried in a cave-in, because some of those tunnels have become unstable with all the houses and roads built over them now. Everyone in Providence has heard about the tunnels and the caves. Most people have never seen them. Some think that they are just a myth. But I grew up being told stories about them and I've done research in the library, and I know they're real. Some of the tunnels and caves were used by abolitionists back in the nineteenth century to hide the runaway slaves who were following the Undergound Railroad north. But they weren't dug then. They are much, much older than that. They're as ancient as one of those nameless things that HPL imagined lurking in the dark, crawling through those tunnels, pushing its way through our creaky old door, coming up the steps one by one. . . .

I tried to keep from thinking about those caves, dark, secret places where almost anything could live. Of course, that is when I finally did fall asleep.

Except I wasn't asleep, or at least I didn't think I was. I just closed my eyes and opened them again. And when I did, I could see myself. I watched myself get up, put on my robe, and go downstairs. I watched my hand reach out to unlock and then open the cellar door. The stairs creaked under my feet, so loud that I was sure everyone in the house—and everything hiding at the bottom of the stairs—could hear.

But it wasn't just the stairs that I heard. I also heard something else, something calling me. It was a whispering voice, a voice so soft that it might have just been my imagination, if I hadn't felt it pulling me with a force I couldn't resist, like iron filings drawn to a magnet.

Child of Canonchet, that spidery voice whispered, *come to me. I am here. I am hungry. I am waiting for you. . . .*

Stop, I told myself. But I kept going down into the darkness. For some reason the lights weren't working. They'd burned out, or we'd had a power failure. I had a flashlight in my hand, though, and I kept playing its beam along the wall. I had to find the fuse box so that I could get the lights back on again.

Then I heard something behind me. I knew that sound. It was the sound of a door, a heavy old door, being slowly opened. I had to turn around, but I couldn't. I knew what I would see looming over me.

I couldn't move. But I could speak. And I said something. I didn't even know that I knew the words in Narragansett until they came out of my mouth. *"Awaun ewo?"* "Who is that?"

"AWAUN EWO?" I shouted the words again as loud as I could. Then hands grabbed me hard by the shoulders.

11

TENSION

UNT LYSSA HAD gone off to the library. Even though it was now the weekend, she liked to work on Saturdays, especially Saturday mornings when things were quiet. She left with her usual smile. Not a word about my three A.M. outburst that woke up her and Roger and brought them both down the hall to my room where they found me standing in front of the closet door with my eyes closed, yelling, "Who is that?" in Narragansett. My aunt had to take me by the shoulders and turn me around before I woke up.

I say that I woke up, but in more ways than one I was still in the middle of that dream. The feeling of dread had been so strong that it hadn't completely left me. I found myself looking over at the door down to the cellar and shuddering more than once while Roger and I ate breakfast. Or at least he ate. All I did was push my food around on my plate. Even though I usually devoured Aunt Lyssa's French toast, my appetite was missing. Grama Delia and my dad had both told me more than once to pay attention to my dreams, because a dream can be a message. But what was the message of that dream, apart from the fact that I was now even more uncertain than I'd been before? Where did those Narragansett words come from? I knew they weren't part of my limited Narragansett vocabulary. It was maddening. I felt as if I knew something, but I didn't know exactly what it was. One thing I did know for sure, though. I had to get out of the house.

I looked over at Roger and he read my mind.

"Want to take a walk?" he said.

I lifted my good hand to wipe the sweat from my brow. It was one of those close, humid days that we get in late summer on the east coast. The sky was hazed over with clouds. It hadn't rained yet, but there was that feeling in the air, like the tension in the head of a drum. Something was going to break soon. A violent storm might come rolling in at any second, roaring up the river, bringing water from the ocean.

"Which way do you want to go, Maddy?"

Roger's voice pulled me out of my reverie, and I looked around. We'd reached the bottom of Benefit Street again, its steep hill rising up toward Brown University. The one-way traffic heading north was thin. The sky and the heavy air around us were still threatening. *Anamakeesuck sokenun.* Soon it will rain. That is what Grama Delia would say in Narragansett.

As soon as I thought that, it reminded me of where those words in my dream probably came from. I didn't remember Grama Delia saying them to me, but I probably just picked them up without knowing it. After all, she'd been teaching me a bunch of words and phrases like that. Ever since I moved to Aunt Lyssa's house after being released from the hospital, Grama Delia had made a point of giving me little language lessons every time she came up from Charlestown for a day or two to visit. She said knowing our language would make me stronger. I wasn't entirely sure what she meant by that. I couldn't see how Indian words could actually protect me. But I loved the feeling of Narragansett on my tongue. Grama Delia doesn't come visit all that often, though. She thinks that Aunt Lyssa is uncomfortable when she sticks around too long.

She's right about that. Aunt Lyssa gets as nervous as a long-tailed cat in a room full of rocking chairs whenever Grama Delia comes to visit. Maybe it is because even though Aunt Lyssa is my closest living relative and my court-appointed guardian, she's still a little uncertain about her role in my life. After all, she never expected to have a stubborn teenager to take care of, especially one obsessed with the supernatural. Sometimes I think she'd be happier just to have her quiet librarian life back again. Other times, though, I think she's really threatened by Indian stuff. Like she's afraid that the more Narragansett things I do and learn, the farther away from her I'll get. Like I'll be stolen by the Indians. Like she felt that my mother—who was her little sister and best friend—was stolen away from her by my father. So I try not to say any Narragansett words around her.

Narragansett words. I don't always feel like I'm

learning them, but then they just pop into my head at times like this. For some reason today is the first time that any of those words have come to me. You don't really hear Narragansett spoken much anymore. I'm not sure if anyone, even Grama Delia, is fluent enough to carry on a long conversation in our old tongue. But unless you live around Charlestown, which has the biggest population of our people in Rogue Island, there's not much likelihood you'll hear any Narragansett spoken at all. That was another thing they made illegal in this state more than a century ago. It was actually against the law for Narragansetts to speak their own language. You had to speak it in secret and pass it on to your children the same way. Of course, nowadays it isn't illegal anymore. My father had always said he was going to teach me our language.

"When?" I'd ask him.

"Soon," he'd say. But he never got around to it.

Kuttannummi nosh. Will you help me, my father?

"What was that you said, Maddy?"

I looked over at Roger. How long had I been speaking my thoughts, mumbling to myself like someone with bipolar disorder, as we walked up Benefit Street?

"Sorry," I said. "I'm just distracted."

"It's okay," Roger said. And he meant it, and I wished that he was right.

12

QUESTIONS

A S ROGER AND I continued to trudge along, I started hoping it would rain. I wanted to hear the thunder roll. *Neimpaug pesk homwak.* Thunder's lightning bolts will strike. That is what you can say about a thunderstorm. *Neimpaug*, that's the thunder. And I love it. Whenever a storm comes rolling up from the coast, I want to sit out on the porch or by the window to watch it come, hoping for thunder and lightning. Aunt Lyssa is freaked out by storms.

"Get back from the windows," she'll say. Or "Don't use the phone during a storm; lightning can come down the wire and kill you."

She even says that about making calls on my cell phone during a storm. It makes me want to laugh the way she gets so scared. But I am careful not to make fun of her. It's not her fault that she's not Indian and doesn't understand the way we think of thunder and lightning. Dad would always smile when he heard the rumble of thunder.

"Old Neimpaug, he's out hunting for monsters," Dad would say. "He's shooting his lightning arrows down at the earth to cleanse the land."

The thunder, though, didn't come. It just stayed hot and humid as we walked, my T-shirt sticking to my back, my hair drooping in heavy, wet curls in front of my eyes. But you could feel that a storm was going to happen. There weren't many people out walking. Still Roger and I kept plodding stubbornly on—or I did, and he stayed by my side. We reached the front of the Governor Hopkins house. Roger took my arm.

"Come on," he said, "let's go sit down." We headed for the terraced garden next to the building.

Roger tried to open the gate, but the latch didn't move.

"Why would they lock up this place on a Saturday morning?" he asked.

"Here," I said, grabbing the latch and jiggling it so that it opened. Maddy, your accomplished tour guide. "This thing always sticks."

We made our way to the bench we had sat on the first time I brought Roger here. It has the best view of the gold dome of the old State bank. For some reason just being able to open that gate made me feel a little less confused and anxious about things. It is funny how familiar things can be so reassuring. The smell of the hedges and the late summer flowers surrounded me, and I took a deep breath.

"Okay," I said to Roger. "Tell me what you're thinking."

Roger put his hand up to his chin and leaned forward to rest his elbow in the palm of his other hand. There was a little smile on his face as he did that, and I knew he was trying to make me smile too, by imitating the pose of a statue. It worked. I actually giggled.

"Okay," he said. "Best way to deal with a monster hungry for your blood is to laugh at it." His face became serious. "No kidding, though, Maddy. Whatever is happening, the worst thing to do is to panic. We gotta really think about what is going on here."

"What is going on here?"

"First of all," he said, "even though I just made you laugh, this is no joke."

'You're right," I agreed. "If it was just the phone calls or the message scratched on my door, it could just be a harmless prank." I poked Roger in the arm. "Like the stuff you and I do to each other sometimes."

Roger grinned briefly. My letters written to him in red ink and signed "Vampira," his phone calls back to me using that Bela Lugosi voice.

"But it's more than that," he said.

"Way beyond that. Because of what was done to Bootsie." I stared at the old bricks of the walkway under my feet. "I think if she hadn't gotten under the shed, she would have been killed."

Roger nodded. "Not just Bootsie. Remember what Mr. Patel said about other dogs being killed?" He stroked his chin again. "I wonder if the blood was drained from their bodies?"

Desite the heat and humidity that was wrapped around us like a blanket, a shiver went down my spine, as if someone had just poured cold water on my back. I didn't want to think any more about this. I wanted to get up and walk away, walk right back into my own everyday life.

The sky was even darker now, and although it was still morning it was almost like twilight. Out in the street, a few of the automatic lights that come on after dark were flickering, as if trying to decide if it was really night already. Then I saw something move out of the corner of my eye.

"What's that?" I said, quickly turning my head.

Roger turned to look with me. "What, Maddy? I didn't see nothin'."

I got up and walked toward the building, toward a window with one pane of glass that looked even older than the others. What I'd seen had not been in front of the building, but almost inside it. I say almost because it looked like a reflection, an image in the bull's-eye pane of glass.

Old windows are strange. They aren't thin and smooth and even like the glass that's been used for the last hundred years. They ripple and distort what they reflect, twisting your vision toward a dimension other than ordinary height and width.

Roger was looking over my shoulder.

"You see that?" I said, reaching my hand toward the pane of glass.

"Jus' a reflection," he said, his voice puzzled.

But it was more than just a reflection of us and the garden in which we stood. The garden in the window was different. The trees and hedges in it were not exactly the same as those behind us. Plus there were people in period clothing strolling in the garden among the late-summer roses. Men wearing beaverskin top hats and carrying canes. Women in long dresses holding parasols over their heads. Had we walked into a set where they were making a film about Providence three centuries ago? I quickly turned to look back into the garden, and Roger turned with me.

"What?" he said.

There was no one behind us. Aside from Roger and me, the terraced garden was completely empty. Was I going crazy? I looked into the window again. This time what I saw rising up behind us made my blood run cold, and I stifled a scream.

❧ 13 ❧

UNDER THE STREET

WHAT DID I see reflected in the window?

It was distorted and foggy, like something you see halfway between a dream and waking up. But it was clear enough. Too clear, in fact. Right behind us, a section of the brick walkway had lifted up. It was like there was a secret trapdoor in the middle of the garden. A red-eyed figure wrapped in darkness was rising out of the ground. I couldn't see the figure's face, but it was lifting one pale arm high as it began to come toward us. There was something held in its raised, threatening hand that glistened like steel. I had to turn around. I had to scream.

But I didn't. Instead I heard words spoken in a voice that started out sounding like my father's and then, I realized, was my own.

Neimpaug pesk homwak.

The strongest gust of wind I have ever felt in my entire life came barreling into the garden at that exact second, along with so much rain that it seemed as if the whole sky was a storm gutter. And with that rain and wind came an arrow of lightning that exploded so close to us it rocked Roger and me back against the side of the building.

We were grabbing onto each other, trying not to fall down, trying to get our bearings. I smelled burning wood, but I could barely see far enough to pick out the ground underfoot. We were stunned and confused by the rain and the concussion of the lightning, and all we could think of was finding shelter. The rain was so heavy that it was barely possible to move as we stumbled forward blindly, and it was absolutely impossible to talk over the roaring, rushing sound of the curtain of rain wrapped tightly around us. It was as if the ocean had come all the way up from the coast and was sending its waves into the town.

Then, as suddenly as it came, it ended. The air cleared and the sky went from black to the milky color of a blown glass bottle. Thunder was still rumbling, but from much farther away. Only that one lightning strike had been close. By the time we'd fumbled our way back to the gate of the garden, we didn't need to find shelter after all.

I wiped rain and hair out of my eyes, gasping like a fish washed up on shore.

"Ohmigod," I said to Roger as I tried to unstick my T-shirt from my body. "Did you see that?"

"Man," he said. "I didn't just see it, I felt it and I smelt it and I darn near drownt in it. I never went through anything like that before." He pointed back at a tree with a black streak down its side and smoke still rising from its roots where the lightning strike grounded. "That bolt didn't hit no more than forty feet away from us. First I thought we were dead, then I thought I was deaf."

Roger lifted his head up toward the sky. "Yahooooo!" he yelled. "You missed us."

I tugged at his sleeve. "No," I said. "I'm not talking about the lightning. The window."

I dragged him back through the garden, where runnels of rain were turning from rivers into small trickling rills, until we stood in front of the old window again.

"In there," I said. "In the glass."

Roger peered close. "Just an old room," he said in a puzzled voice.

I looked at the window myself. This time it didn't give back any reflection at all. I could see right through its warped glass into the small back room with pictures on the walls, a table, and a few chairs.

I turned to study the brick walkway, trying to pick out the exact spot that I thought I'd seen.

"Right here," I said to Roger. "I saw this part of the garden reflected in that window like it was a mirror. And there was like a trapdoor here. The brick sidewalk lifted up and something or someone was coming out of it. Am I crazy?"

I started to turn away, but Roger caught hold of my sleeve.

"Maddy, look at that."

He bent down to look close and gave a low whistle through his teeth. There, sticking out from between two water-washed bricks of the walkway, wedged in so deeply that we could not pull it free, was the broken, upside-down stem of a rose.

14

KNIFE HAND

I T ISN'T EASY at times being Indian. I know I'm half white, but it doesn't make the Indian part of me any less. Plus I look Indian. My skin is dark, my eyes are slanted, and my hair is thick and black. My dad used to say that all I had to do was put on a buckskin dress to look just like a Narragansett girl from the seventeenth century.

But I live in these times, times when people find Indians interesting but sort of quaint. Modern-day people claim to be rational—even though they believe in urban legends and their kids all read the Harry Potter books and dream about being wizards. So if you start talking Indian stuff as if you really believe it, they may just look at you as if they pity you for believing crap like that. And if you talk about the past, a lot of people say you should just forget it. Live in the present day. Whatever happened, happened. This is the twenty-first century. Forget about it. But Indians don't forget. I might listen to Eminem on my Walkman and play video games and send e-mail, but that doesn't make me a different person. It doesn't change the beat of my heart. We Indians know what century we are living in, but we also remember how we got here. And we remember the stories created along the way.

"Roger," I said, "I have to tell you about the Whisperer in the Dark."

"You mean that old story about the Indian boogeyman," Roger said. "You told me that one already, Maddy."

"No," I said. "Not really."

"You mean there's more to it than just some monster that takes away kids who've been bad?" Roger said, trying to make light of it. Then he saw the look on my face and stopped. "Sorry, Mad," he said. "Go ahead."

"I didn't tell you the whole story," I said. "The Whisperer story isn't just one of those Narragansett tales that is as ancient as our hills. Part of it also comes from the time after the arrival of the Knife

Men. *Chauquacock*. That's the name my Indian ancestors gave to the English. Some say it was because they admired the Europeans' blades that were not made of wood or bone or flint like our knives, but fashioned out of some new, hard, and shiny substance with sharp edges. My dad, though, said we also gave the English that name because those newcomers could sometimes be just as hard and cold and dangerous as the weapons they carried."

Roger settled back against the stone and crossed his arms. He could tell I was in my Maddy the Historian mode and that my story was going to take a while. I took a deep breath.

"Anyhow, the story of the Whisperer is like a lot of things that are Narragansett now but have a kind of English influence to them. Like the way the Narragansetts greeted Roger Williams when he first arrived here to found Providence, way back in 1636. 'What cheer, *netop*,' they said to him. *Netop* means 'friend' in the Narragansett language. But 'what cheer' was the way that English people greeted each other back then. Sort of like 'Whassup?' now. The Narragansetts had learned those words from the early English traders."

I explained to Roger how I had gotten so freaked out by Grama Delia's story about the Whisperer in the Dark that it was a long time before I figured I was finally ready to hear more. But this time I went to my dad. Dad was so strong, so big and solid, that it was safer to hear such a scary story from him. Back then I thought he would always be around to protect me. Dad was always ready to talk about our ways. It was one of the things we always used to do together. So when I asked him about the Whisperer, he just put aside the wood carving he'd been working on, pulled his stool away from the bench, and sat me on his lap.

"The Whisperer," he said. "You want to know about that scary monster, Maddy girl?"

"Uh-huh," I said, clasping my hands together and leaning back against his broad chest.

Then Dad told me what he'd heard as a kid. No one really knew what that creature looked like. But they were afraid, terribly afraid of hearing its cold voice. Because when you heard the Whisperer speak, that meant that it had chosen you. It didn't come right out and grab you like a corny movie monster. You first heard its voice four different times. The fourth time was when it finally spoke your name. Then you had to go to it. You couldn't stop yourself. After that you were never ever seen again.

Having my big, strong father tell me what he knew about the Whisperer actually made me feel a little better. Sure, it was spooky stuff, but with Dad right there to protect me, I knew I had nothing to worry about. I knew he was going to pick up where Grama Delia's story about the Whisperer left off and tell me how that monster was defeated. And, sure enough, he did.

"Finally," Dad continued, "the people decided they had to do something. The Whisperer had preyed on too many of their loved ones, and they had to put a stop to him. So one night they surrounded the part of the dark swamp near the coast where it was said the Whisperer lived. The people all had torches and made a great ring of fire. Fire and the bright light of the sun were the only things the monster feared. They kept moving in closer and closer. They saw a shadow slipping through the trees, running away from them, away from that fire.

They drove it back up the hill to a cave in a steep cliff where they knew it would take shelter from the light. Sure enough it did, and when they lifted their torches to see what was in the cave, what some of them saw was even more awful than they had expected. They blocked up the mouth of that cave with big stones and piled earth on top of that. They put down strong medicine to keep anyone or anything from opening it. That medicine was supposed to last for a thousand seasons. For a long time after that, no one heard the Whisperer in the Dark."

"What did they see?" I asked.

Dad smiled. "I knew you were going to ask that, Maddy. Although they saw it only briefly, although it was covered with the blood of his victims, they thought they recognized the monster's face. It was the face of one of their own people, the pawwaw who had been hungry for power before he had disappeared many seasons earlier. An evil spirit had come into him, and he had become a monster. When they closed that cave, they meant to seal in not just that man, but also the spirit that had turned him into something inhuman."

But, I told Roger, that was not the end of what my dad shared with me.

"What your Grama Delia didn't tell you," my father said, "is that the Whisperer in the Dark returned many years later, after the coming of the English during the time of Canonchet. This time that dark spirit didn't choose to inhabit one of our people. Instead it chose an Englishman. You could say that made sense. None of our monsters were as dangerous as the English. The long-ago monsters just killed a few people every now and then. But the English seemed to want to destroy all the Indians. We discovered that if we wanted to scare our kids into behaving right, it was a lot more effective to tell them the Chauquacock, those English Knife Men, were going to get them, than to say they'd be taken away by a giant bird or some other Indian monster."

There was, my father explained, one Chauquaco, one Knife Man, in particular. He was the most bloodthirsty of all the English. Even the other Englishmen feared him. He was a soldier who had fought not just our people, but native people in other parts of the world. Asia, Africa, the islands of the Pacific. Wherever he went, he took delight in killing—not just other warriors, but those who were weak, like children and elders. Then he drank their blood because he said it made him stay strong. His hair was white, but he didn't look old. His eyes were red, and his skin was as pale as something you'd find under a rock. He was fearless in battle, and not just because he wore an armor-plated vest so that spears and arrows just bounced off him. He was huge and powerful. The only thing that he seemed wary of was bright light, and so he always attacked at twilight or in the dark. He had become like an animal, living in the woods apart from the rest of the English. Because he preyed only on the Indians, his own people left him alone.

We Narragansetts had a name for him. It was Chauquaco Wunnicheke, which means "Knife Hand," because he carried a vicious weapon. It was a five-bladed knife with a handle. When he gripped it, those blades stuck out from his fist like razor-sharp claws.

One night our warriors took Knife Hand captive. They came upon him crouched like a wolf over the body of a young man he had killed. He was drinking the blood. When he looked up, he saw a circle of men. Half of them held torches, while the others kept their arrows pointed at his heart. His red eyes gleamed as he tried to shrink away from the light, but they had encircled him and he couldn't escape.

Some wanted to execute him right on the spot.

"*Nissnissoke*," some of our men said. "Kill him like a dog."

"A quick end is too good," others said. "Let him know the long death of many wounds."

But Canonchet did not agree.

"A warrior's death is too good for this one," he said.

They stripped Knife Hand of his armor and his weapons. Then they took him to a cave in the side of a nearby cliff. It was not a place where people ever went because it was said that a powerful bad *Chepi*, a spirit-being, dwelled there. The cave's mouth had been sealed with great stones and medicine a thousand seasons before. It was the same cave where the Whisperer had been buried alive.

"Open the cave," Canonchet said.

So the stones were pried out of the mouth of the

cave. Then they shoved the Knife-handed One into the darkness. Strangely he did not resist them, but went into that darkness as if he knew it, as if it was his own, as if he was eager to join it. Then the Narragansett men closed up the mouth of that cave again, tighter than before. But before they wedged the last stones in place, Canonchet threw that five-bladed knife in through the hole.

"Use this to cut your own throat," Canonchet said.

Knife Hand, though, remained defiant. The last words that they heard him speak before they closed the hole were not shouted or screamed. They were whispered in a voice that chilled the spirits of all those who heard, not just for what was said, but because those words were spoken not in English but in their own tongue, in Narragansett.

"I will not die here," he whispered. "The seasons will pass, and I will return again. I will come back for your children."

I took a deep breath. For a moment it had been as if I was standing there with Canonchet, putting the last stone into the mouth of that cave, not in modern-day Providence with cars and busses going by only fifty yards away.

"'I will come back for your children,'" I said. "That's what the Whisperer in the Dark said to Canonchet. Canonchet, my ancestor. And remember my bad dream from last night? I heard a voice in my dream, a voice that drew me to it. The voice called me Child of Canonchet, and it said it was waiting for me. And just now, in the reflection of the window, I saw him. The Whisperer in the Dark."

I looked down at the stone pavement under our feet. Was Roger going to laugh at what I'd just told him? Was he going to say it was silly for me to worry about a made-up bloodthirsty monster from hundreds of years ago? Even though he was big into horror fiction and worshipped Anne Rice, it didn't mean he really believed any of that. It was probably all just fantasy for him. "A safe escape from the pressures of the modern world," as his mother might say in one of her lectures at Brown.

Sure, I'd told Roger some of our Narragansett stories before, but never like I believed them. Never like I was sure there really was something out there waiting to get me. I'd always kept this cool facade going. I was in control. Maddy, the mistress of all she surveys. But for the last twenty-four hours, I'd been crumbling like an old wall whose mortar has worn out. If Roger laughed at me, or told me to grow up and get real, it would all come down, every last stone. I'd be totally exposed and all alone. And then what would I do? Maybe I would just run and keep running.

Roger reached out a long finger to tuck back a thick strand of damp hair that had come coiling down over my eye. It was the sort of thing my mother used to do. It was so kind and gentle that it made me raise my head to look at him. He didn't say a word, but just nodded. Then he slid his arm down to put it around my shoulder. I let out a sob and just grabbed at him. I wrapped my own arms around his skinny waist, my good hand grabbing my other wrist. I held on to Roger like a shipwrecked sailor holds on to a floating timber.

I imagine that people who saw us standing there like that thought we were just a couple of exhibitionist kids who were making out in public. But we were two friends, real friends who could depend on each other. And as I hugged Roger, he seemed as solid and reliable as a tree.

Our Narragansett creation story says that Cautantowwit made the first people from stone, but then broke them up and put them back into the earth because they were hard-hearted and uncaring. Then Cautantowwit shaped a man and a woman from the ash tree, and when those first people stepped forth they were as connected to the earth and as graceful and giving as the beautiful trees. That was how I felt as I stood there holding on to Roger—safe and rooted as we swayed a little bit like two trees in the wind.

That moment didn't last long. We both stepped back, just a little embarrassed, but glad that we'd had that moment.

We turned together and began to walk down Benefit Street.

I was the first to break the silence. "What do you think?" I said.

Roger stopped walking. "At first, everything that's happening seemed like a bunch of unconnected things: the random phone calls, the words scratched into your door, and then, most serious of all, Bootsie getting injured. But now, after what just happened back there, together with your dream . . . if it really *is* the Whisperer, why now?"

I bit my lip. "Maybe after all these years, it finally got out of that cave. There's always construction going on and things being dug up."

"Like in that movie where they find a dragon egg."

"*Reign of Fire*, but that's just a takeoff on the Japanese movies where nuclear tests wake up something ancient and ominous."

"*Godzilla*, which my mom says is just a Japanese parable about the dangers of nuclear weapons destroying the world."

"Which," I continued, putting on my professor's voice, "in itself is just a modern version of Mary Shelley's *Frankenstein*, wherein our monsters are just models of the worst part of our human selves, and science doesn't necessarily make anything better."

We stood there, nodding our heads and feeling pleased with ourselves, as if we'd actually figured something out and not just worked our way back into our familiar routine of talking about scary creatures. Except this wasn't a senior-high seminar on monster motifs in film and fiction.

"Except for the fact," Roger said, reading my mind again.

"That this is real," I concluded.

Roger sighed. "Maddy," he said, shaking his head, "whatever way you look at it, we got real trouble."

15

GOOD COURAGE

AM NOT SURE when we started running. Maybe
I said something about our jogging some to dry
off from the rainstorm. All I know is that running
was the only thing that made sense to me just then
and so I ran, legs thumping the pavement in a sweet,
even rhythm, my heartbeat as steady and strong as
the pumping muscles in my calves and thighs and
hips. Running.

No matter how far you run, you can't escape fate.
Grama Delia had said that to me once.

The memory of her words shot through my head
like a poison dart. It made me stumble and almost
fall. I slowed down to a jog and Roger slowed with
me until the two of us were walking, our hands on
our hips, taking measured breaths. Even though
it was still hot, the storm had cleared some of the

mugginess from the air. We hadn't run that far, only about five K. Neither one of us was anywhere close to winded. But I knew that no matter how far I ran, even if I ran a hundred miles through the mountains like the Tarahumara Indians of Mexico do, I couldn't manage to run away from what was after me.

I looked around to get my bearings. We'd been running along Riverwalk, next to the Woonasquatucket River. We'd stopped by the amphitheater near the tunnel that leads from Riverwalk to Kennedy Plaza and the center of downtown Providence. I looked at the tunnel.

Roger came up next to me. "I don't think I want to go through there either," he said. "Not under the ground, even though it's a new tunnel and probably safe. The hidden tunnels, like the ones Lovecraft wrote about, they're all old ones."

I nodded my head. I knew Roger was remembering the same stories I was. Like "The Rats in the Walls," with giant cannibal caverns under an ancestral castle. But then there was also that picture Lovecraft describes in another story that showed horrible fanged creatures attacking people at a subway station.

"No, I don't want to go into that tunnel," I said.

"No way," Roger said, drawing his finger across his throat.

"This is crazy."

"I know," Roger agreed. "But we both saw the rose, stuck there in between those bricks as if there was a trapdoor there."

We began to walk, my good hand holding the numb fingers of my other hand cupped against my diaphragm. I had a sick feeling in my stomach again. Next to us the river flowed on as always, as if nothing was wrong with the world. I found myself wishing a birch-bark canoe would come floating up to us. A Narragansett man dressed in the traditional way would be in it, holding a carved paddle and smiling up at us.

Comishoohom? he would say. "Do you want to go by water?"

I would want to say *Nux*, which means "yes," and get into that canoe and let him paddle me far away from all my fear and uncertainty. But I would shake my head.

Machaug, I said. "No, not now." I can't just save myself and leave everyone else behind.

He smiled again, the same broad smile I remember on my father's face.

Maumaneeteantass, netop.

Then he turned back to his paddling, the heavy muscles of his shoulders and his broad back rippling as he worked the paddle, pushing his way swiftly up that river against the current until he was out of sight.

I felt a smile coming on to my face as I stood there looking at the empty river.

"Maddy," Roger said, "what were you saying just then? You talking Indian?"

"*Maumaneeteantass, netop,*" I said slowly. "Be of good courage, my friend."

Roger nodded his head. "I like that. When did you learn that?"

"I don't know that I ever heard it," I said, "until just now."

I sat down on a bench and patted the seat beside me. Roger folded himself down, put one arm over the back of the bench, crossed his leg, right ankle over left knee, and turned to give me his full attention.

"Tell me what you think," I said.

Roger cupped his chin with his hand and slowly shook his head back and forth. "I don't know what I think. I mean, we're always reading these stories and seeing the movies and talking about things like this. And we're always saying things like we wouldn't be that stupid to go into the woods like him or to go up into the attic like her, or to split up like those two did when they were searching the haunted house for whatever made that scary noise, you know? But I never really thought about any of it actually being real."

"Me too," I said.

"But it is. Maybe that monster, that Whisperer in the Dark, has come back and it has chosen you because, like you say, you are Narragansett and one of the last real descendants of Ca-ca-"

"Canonchet," I said.

"Canonchet. Or maybe it is just some crazy man, one of those serial killers, who has put you in his sights. And there wouldn't have to be any real reason for him to choose you or for that to happen apart from the fact that people like that don't need to have any reasons to do that sort of thing."

Roger's voice grew slower as he reached the end

of his sentence, almost the way a windup toy slows down and then stops because all of the energy in it has run out. He was quiet for a while. Then he took a deep breath, let it out, and sat up straighter.

"Should we go to the police?"

"What do we tell them?" I said. "I got two prank phone calls, my dog got scratched up, we got caught in a rainstorm, and now I am convinced that a serial killer or some razor-handed monster out of a Narragansett legend is coming to get me? They'll either get ticked off at us for trying to put them on, or they'll think we're on drugs, or they'll just patiently shake their heads and tell us it's just our overactive imaginations. This city is such a weird place with a crazy history. They're used to wacky stories like this. Witches, vampires, werewolves, blobs from outer space. Par for the course in Providencesylvania. Plus we're teenagers, remember? In a policeman's dictionary *teenager* is just another word for 'pain-in-the-neck troublemaker.'"

"I guess you're right," Roger said, slumping back on the bench.

"I remember," I said, "this show I saw on the Discovery Channel about how hyenas hunt. A hyena will just walk through a whole herd of animals until it sees the one animal it wants. Maybe it's a gazelle that is lame or weaker than the others. But when it chooses that gazelle, that is the only one it goes after. It keeps after it without even looking to the right or left. It keeps after it, no matter how fast that gazelle runs. It just keeps after it until it catches it."

Roger looked at me. "Maddy," he said, "that don't sound like you. You saying you gonna give up?"

I shook my head. "No," I said, hearing how stubborn the tone of my voice was just then and not minding it at all. "I just mean that running away won't save me. *Maumaneeteantass*. I am not going to try to run away."

16

CALLING

∞

YOU KNOW HOW it is when you've been uncertain about something. Should I do this? Should I do that?

It doesn't have to be anything that big, maybe just what top to wear to school or which show to tape and which one to watch live, whether to go to the movies or go for a run. But while you're not sure what to do you feel all antsy, as if nothing is quite right in the whole world.

I know I'm using dumb examples, but that is how life is sometimes. Lots of little hassles can seem big unless you have something like a real threat to your continued existence to put things into perspective. Then you finally make up your mind and everything seems clearer, as if the sun finally came out again after a week of rainy skies.

That was how it was with me when I made up my mind not to run away, but to find some way to confront whatever it was that was out there. But now that I'd made that decision, I had another problem. What exactly *was* I going to do?

Roger wondered the same thing. I could tell by the way he looked at me, waiting for my brilliant solution. Which was not forthcoming.

"Maddy," Roger said, putting his hand up to his chin. "I've been wondering about somethin'. Do you think whoever or whatever it is would try to get to you in another way? They already got to Bootsie. Would they try to contact anyone else in your family?"

"Aunt Lyssa," I said. "Omigod!"

I unzipped my hip pack, yanked out my phone, fumbled it open, and hit the numbers for Aunt Lyssa's desk at the library. It rang four times, and then I heard her voice.

"I'm not here or I'm on the other line. You can leave a message after—"

I broke the connection and looked over at Roger.

"Want to go there and check on her?" he said.

I had the number for the taxi company where Mr. Patel worked stored in the memory. The cheerful voice of the dispatcher answered on the second ring.

"This is Madeline Brown," I said. "I am at the amphitheater on Riverwalk and I need a taxi."

"Hi, Madeline," the familiar voice said. "Mrs. Jenkins here."

Mrs. Jenkins. I knew her voice, but that was all. You know how it is with those telephone voices you get to know. They belong to people you have called before for some business reason, but you've never met them in person.

"Hi, Mrs. Jenkins," I said.

"So where you going today?"

"Just to the library."

There was a pause on the other end. "Far be it from me to turn away business, Madeline, but it'd be faster for you to just walk there from where you are. All you have to do is walk through the tunnel."

NO. I almost yelled that into the phone. NOT the tunnel. But I controlled myself. "I, uh, I was out running and hurt my foot. Just a little. So I really need a taxi. Really."

"Not a problem," Mrs. Jenkins chirped. "Patel, your pal, is the closest cab. He'll be there in ten."

It was actually seven minutes. While we were waiting, I tried twice more to call Aunt Lyssa and got her voice mail each time. I didn't bother to call back to the desk and see if they knew where she was. I'd be there myself in almost no time. I flipped my phone closed and stowed it back in my hip pack.

Then Roger and I sat without talking, just waiting. I do a lot of talking, but there are some people I can be quiet around. Roger is one. Grama Delia is another. Her silences always say so much. At times when I am with her and we are both not talking, it is like she is teaching me by speaking mind to mind, not with words, but with emotions. I wished I could talk with Grama Delia now. She'd probably know just the right thing to tell me. But I knew that she wasn't home. She wasn't even in Rhode Island. And I had no idea what city in New Mexico she was in for the Native American Elders' Conference this week.

I closed my eyes, picturing Grama Delia's confident, compassionate face. She has seen so much in her life, and every line in her face is a sign of knowledge she has earned. She says that we Indians can talk to each other when we are far away. We just need to use our minds and really focus. Telephone and e-mail and all the modern ways of communicating have made it harder for the old telepathy to work, but it is still possible. Reach for that person in your mind the right way, and then you hear a voice calling your name.

"Maddy."

Mr. Patel leaned the whole top half of his slender body out of the window of his cab and waved at me with both hands as he called my name a second time. In the five years I've known Mr. Patel, ever since he came here from Bombay, I've never seen him completely outside of his taxicab. I've never even seen him open his driver's-side door. It's not like he can't walk. It is just that he prefers doing the most amazing contortions through his window to actually opening the door and getting out. I remember one day when he slid out his window with the boneless ease of an acrobat to open the back door and then help me wrestle a big box into the backseat. It was only later that I realized, while thinking back on it, that he had done it with one leg on the street and the other still inside the taxi. I've heard, though it may not be true, that he is a yoga teacher in his spare time.

"Come on, you two," Mr. Patel said, gesturing toward the back door of his cab with hands as fluid as those of a temple dancer. "Your humble chariot awaits you."

I had to smile. "Let's go," I said, poking Roger in the side to get him moving. He was sitting there as if hypnotized.

"Maddy," Roger whispered to me. "Is it safe to ride with this guy again? You didn't see how he just drove up here. He was steering with his bare feet and his hands behind his head."

"It's okay. I think he's the safest driver in Providence. He even uses turn signals."

Roger got up. "All right then," he said.

The turn signals remark, which was true, had made an impression on him. Roger had been back in Rogue Island long enough to become fully aware of another of the idiosyncrasies of our peculiar little state. Almost nobody ever uses their turn signals. There is even a famous cartoon I have seen that shows a Rhode Island used-car salesman with a customer. "And the turn signals on this are just as good as new," the caption reads. Rhode Islanders roar when they see the cartoon, but out-of-staters just shake their heads in confusion.

Mr. Patel reached his long arm back to shut the door after us, then spun around to face us. "So, so, so," he said, "it is good to see you so soon again. How is your Bootsie?"

For a few seconds, I'd forgotten about the awful things that had happened or seemed about to happen. But his question brought it all back, and it showed on my face.

"Oh," he said, "I am sorry. The news is bad?"

"No," I said quickly. "Bootsie is fine. Dr. Fox is going to keep her for a couple of days."

"Ah, ah," Mr. Patel said. "Wonderful." He flicked his turn signal, looked to his left, and then pulled out from the curb. "Library?"

"Yes, that's where we're going."

Mr. Patel pulled up smoothly to the light, looked both ways, flipped his right turn signal, and eased the cab around the corner. I looked over at Roger and he nodded back at me. I hadn't been exaggerating about either Mr. Patel's driving or his use of turn signals.

"At last some good news about this attacking of dogs and domestic animals," Mr. Patel said. "Now if they would only catch the miscreant. But such disturbed persons are often hard to apprehend. If indeed this one is disturbed and not following some darker purpose. In some ways it puts me in mind of a Thug, one of those awful people we used to have in India who killed and stole for the goddess Kali as a part of their religious practices. But then"—Mr. Patel flicked his left turn signal and eased his way into downtown Providence—"they murdered their human victims by strangling with a silken cord, not by cutting off heads."

A shiver ran down my back. "Excuse me," I said, "did you say cutting off heads?"

"Oh my, yes," Mr. Patel said. "Did I not mention it before? All of the other unfortunate animals that were attacked were decapitated and the blood drained from their bodies. Most gruesome."

17

WEAKNESS

HEADS. AND NOT only had they been cut off the bodies of the dozen or so dogs and cats that had been killed over the last few days, they'd also been missing. Which meant that whoever cut them off took the heads with him. It sent my mind back to one of the more gruesome customs of some of my own ancestors.

One of the pictures that you often get in history books and movies about Indians is that of scalping redskins. Maybe not so much nowadays, but plenty of stuff still has that image. Like any John Wayne western. But anybody who knows much about our real history knows that scalping either didn't exist or was really rare among the Indians before Europeans came. But after the British and the French got here, and brought their wars with them, things changed. Maybe Europeans didn't invent scalping, but they made it big business. The colonial governments paid bounties for Indian scalps, and there were bands of white men back in the eighteenth century who made their living as scalp hunters. And those Indian scalps were sold on the street corners in London and Paris to people who bought them as collector's items.

But before you think I'm just going off on a rant about the awful things that white people brought, let me finish where I'm going with this. Heads. In battle, my dad told me, we Narragansetts sometimes took the heads of our enemies as trophies. And the Whisperer in the Dark was also supposed to do that. The story goes that when he killed his victims, after he drank their blood, he would take their heads with him.

That is why Mr. Patel's remark shook me up so much. I know it bothered Roger, too, but only because it was just another gruesome detail. To me, though, it was like hearing a heavy footstep in the hall late at night just outside your door when you thought you were all alone in the house.

I don't recall much more of the conversation

during our short ride to the library. The next thing I knew, Roger was paying our fare and the two of us were standing on the curb outside Mr. Patel's cab.

"Remember, Maddy," he called back to us over his shoulder as he leaned out the passenger side window, "if you need help, just call for Patel." He grinned broadly. "We Indians must stick close together."

Then, like a woodchuck ducking into its hole, he dropped back onto his seat. With a ceremonious gesture, he flicked on his left turn signal and pulled out into traffic.

"You sure were right, Maddy," Roger said, watching the taillight on the cab flash. "He does use those signals."

I didn't say anything. I was still too upset at what Mr. Patel had told us.

"We have to check on Aunt Lyssa," I said, running up the stairs.

But even though I was running, I was still trying to think. I had to be logical, even if everything that was happening seemed to defy normal logic. Our traditional stories were meant not just as entertainment. They taught survival lessons. One of the

major lessons is to keep calm when there is danger. That way you won't run headlong into the jaws of whatever is threatening you, like a panicked jackrabbit running in a big circle right back to the place it started from. When you are calm, you can think. My mom once told me that is how my dad was when he served in the military over in the Middle East. He was a Marine. When his convoy got ambushed, my dad was the one who stayed cool, figured out where the ambush was coming from, and led the assault team that took out the enemies. That earned him a Silver Star.

Stay calm. Think logically. I could do that.

I pushed through the library door and looked around. Aunt Lyssa was not at the front desk, but that wasn't unusual. She was probably in her office. Everything was okay. I didn't have to hurry. I had to calm down. I had to think.

I stepped back into a corner and lowered myself into a cross-legged position. Roger sat down next to me, waiting patiently without saying a word.

If—and I knew it was a really big *if*—I really was being stalked by the Whisperer in the Dark, I had to stop running. I had to start thinking. Grama

Delia always told me that one of the most important lessons is that everything evil has a weakness. In fact, it isn't just that way in our tales, but stories from all over the world. It's true even in the more modern books and movies that are such an obsession for Roger and me. A wooden stake in the heart destroys Dracula. A silver bullet wipes out the Wolf Man. Every monster can be overcome if you know the right way to go about it. That lightning strike back at the Governor Hopkins house had reminded me of one of the weaknesses of what might be stalking me. And it tied right into the stories told to me by Grama Delia and my dad. Fire and bright light. In both their stories, the Whisperer in the Dark could not stand to be out in the bright light of day.

I began to make a mental list of all the things we owned that could be useful. The strobe flash on my digital camera. The halogen beams of the big flashlights that we keep in different rooms in case the power goes out. Then there were the boxes of matches in the kitchen cupboard that we use to start the wood fires in our fireplace insert. But all of those were back at my house. I didn't even have a penlight or a match on me. I've never smoked or even wanted to, but at that moment I wished I was one of those kids who carried a butane cigarette lighter.

I needed something, something I could have with me as soon as possible. Then I remembered the laser pointer that Aunt Lyssa keeps in her office. Perfect.

"Come on," I said to Roger, standing up without touching my hands to the floor.

It's a convenient skill to have when you've got one good hand to rely on. I learned how to spin to my feet from a cross-legged position from taking some of Aunt Lyssa's martial arts classes.

I strode down the hall toward Aunt Lyssa's office with Roger half a step behind me. I was in the lead again and back to my old self. I had a plan and felt so much better because of it. I still wasn't sure that I was going to tell Aunt Lyssa anything about the Whisperer in the Dark, of course. But I could slip that laser pointer off her desk and get it safely stowed in my hip pack. We got on the elevator and I pressed the button for Aunt Lyssa's floor.

"Just follow my lead," I said to Roger.

"As if I had any choice," he replied with a little smile, the first real one he'd cracked since the day before when we took Bootsie to Doc Fox.

We hadn't solved anything, not really, but we both felt as if we had turned a corner. I was even humming as we got off the elevator and headed for the administrative corridor.

But when we rounded the corner and reached Aunt Lyssa's office door, we found another unpleasant surprise waiting for us.

The door to Aunt Lyssa's office was shut. I knew I would find it locked even before I attempted to turn the knob. The only time my aunt's office door was ever closed was when she was gone for the day. Aunt Lyssa is one of those people who lives her life like an open book. Plus she adores visitors and loves to talk. Even when she's out to lunch or at a meeting somewhere else in the building, that door of hers is kept open. People usually gather around her doorway—if not to chat with my aunt then to see what new cartoons about libraries and librarians she has posted on her door under her treasured picture of Conan the Librarian.

It wasn't just the locked door that told us my

aunt was gone, but also her note. It was not in her usual neat writing, but had been hastily printed on a sheet of yellow lined paper pulled so quickly from her notepad that the top edge was roughly torn.

FAMILY
EMERGENCY
HAD TO GO

I stood there, staring stupidly at the closed door. What emergency? Even though I knew Aunt Lyssa wasn't there, I felt like I needed desperately to go inside. I'm not sure why, but I just had that feeling. Could I locate Fred, the janitor, and ask him to open it? Could I open it with a credit card like people do all the time in corny detective shows on television? Then I remembered the key ring in my hip pack and felt even more stupid. Not only did I have the keys to our house's front and back doors on it, I had Aunt Lyssa's spare key to her office. I fumbled with the lock, the fingers of my right hand almost as wooden and stupid as those on my left.

Finally the key turned. Roger and I burst in through the door.

Of course there was nothing unusual to be seen in the office. No movie cliche "signs of a struggle" or bodies on the floor. No broken windows, no bloody handprints, no strange primitive statues of winged and tentacled monsters, no trails of alien slime on the walls. Just the usual friendly clutter of books and catalogs piled on just about every available flat surface.

Then something caught my eye. In the midst of all her clutter, my aunt always keeps the top of her desk neat. So I immediately noticed another piece of yellow lined paper with my aunt's writing on it in the middle of her desk by the phone.

Aunt Lyssa has never been one to record messages word for word. She has this sort of shorthand method, taking down every tenth word or so. In this case she'd written:

> M
> trouble
> not bad
> resting
> Come home

Roger leaned over my shoulder and slowly read the note aloud.

"I don't get it," he said.

I studied the note. There was the letter *M* at the top of the sheet. *M* for Maddy. It could only mean that my aunt had been told by someone that I was in trouble. But how could that be?

I suddenly realized, like a punch in the gut, that someone—or something—could have called my aunt and deceived her, convinced her that she needed to come right home.

Aunt Lyssa's phone is a direct line to her desk. It doesn't come through the library switchboard. I grabbed the receiver and stabbed in *69 so hard that I broke the nail on my index finger.

"The number of your last incoming call was . . ." the pleasant mechanical voice began.

Then it said the number. My home number. The number of our house, where the Whisperer in the Dark was waiting.

~ 18 ~
THE LAST CALL

"ROGER," I SAID, the tone of my voice just short of panic, "we've got to get to my house. My number, the last call Aunt Lyssa answered, was from my house. Get it?"

Roger got it. His face became pale. "It called her," he said.

"Hel-lo," said a voice from the doorway. Roger and I were both so keyed up that we jumped a mile and snapped our heads around so fast to look at the door that we almost gave ourselves whiplash.

It was Fred, the janitor.

"Who's your friend, Maddy?" Fred said.

"Roger," I said, half a second before Roger said the same thing. Our two tense voices made his name sound like an echo bouncing back from a canyon wall.

Fred smiled. "Pleased to meet you, Roger-oger. Anything wrong?"

"Nothing," we both answered, in perfect nervous unison.

Fred raised an eyebrow. "Obviously," he said in a dry voice. "In any circumstance, Maddy, if you're looking for your aunt, you just missed her. I saw her depart the building a mere ten minutes ago."

"Thanks," I said, jumping up and hurling myself through the door.

"Pleased," Roger said as he brushed by Fred, "to meet you."

I was all the way outside on the sidewalk and just about to break into a frantic dash for home when Roger caught up with me and grasped my shoulder.

"Wait," he said.

"I can't," I said, reaching up to tear his arm away. As I did so I realized that I had been holding something in my hand. It was Aunt Lyssa's laser pointer. I'd grabbed it off the desk without thinking at the exact moment when Fred startled us in the office.

"Listen," Roger said, "we've got to be calm, right?" He took the laser pointer that I had almost stabbed him with out of my hand.

"Right," I said.

"So let's think about the best thing to do right now. Your aunt didn't bring her car to work, right?"

Was that right? My brain didn't seem to want to function, like a computer with some new, unnamed virus. I searched my memory and saw Aunt Lyssa's blue Honda parked in the driveway next to our house. It had been there this morning after she left for work. Aunt Lyssa had walked. I remember her saying that it was such a beautiful day and it wasn't that far, almost exactly five K, to the library from our door. Of course the weather had changed by mid-morning. Even though it wasn't raining now, storm clouds were still overhead.

"Right," I said. I thought I saw where Roger was going now.

"So she wouldn't have a quick way home. But even if it didn't look like rain, once she got that message that you were hurt and resting at home, she'd want to get home as fast as she could."

I nodded.

"So unless she got a friend from the library to drive her, she probably called a cab to pick her up on the street. Fred said he saw her go out the door alone. So that probably means she decided to get a cab. We both know it takes a while for a cab to come, so there's a good chance she's not even home yet. But there's no way we can get there first by running. So what can we do to get there as fast as possible?" Roger held out his arm and pointed up the street. "I say we call a cab now and ask them to pick us up somewhere between here and your house. Then we start running like hell toward that rendezvous point."

My fingers were already dialing the number of the taxi company. Mrs. Jenkins answered at the first ring.

"Providence Taxi."

"It's Maddy," I said. "Can you get a cab to pick us up as quick as possible at . . ." I thought for a moment, pictured the cross streets that were about a third of the way to my home, and then blurted out their names.

"Maddy," Mrs. Jenkins said, her voice concerned. "What's wrong?"

"I don't have time to tell you," I said. "I've just got to get home right away. We'll be running from the direction of the library. Okay?"

Roger and I were already starting to jog down the street as I spoke those last words. I snapped the phone shut, shoved it in my hip pack, and we broke into a finish-line sprint.

∾ 19 ∾

RUNNING

RUNNING. MY MOM used to say that I started trying to run when I was only able to crawl. I would get up on my toes and my hands, sort of in a stance like a lineman in football, and scoot forward as fast as I could. When I finally did get up, it wasn't to take tentative steps, but to hurl myself forward, no matter what was in my way. Fortunately it was usually my mom or dad ready to catch me before I hurt myself.

By the time I was in first grade, I was such a fast runner that none of the other kids could keep up with me on the playground. In fact, I remember one day in second grade. During gym class out on the ball field, some of the other kids were teasing me about my hair, which was always thick and dark. I hadn't figured out how to style it in those days, and so it was always kind of matted together back then. This one boy started saying my hair looked like a doormat.

"Madeline's a doormat," he chanted, "Madeline's a doormat."

Naturally the other kids took up that chant. Some kids would have cried at being picked on like that. What I did was to push that boy so hard that he fell right on his butt. Then I took off. My gym teacher tried to catch me, but even though his legs were three times as long as mine, I left him in the dust. When I reached the fence, I crawled over it like a squirrel, hit the ground on the other side, and just kept running.

By the time I got home, I was so sweaty that my hair was no longer matted but hung down around my eyes in wet curls. I wasn't angry anymore either. I had run all the anger out of me. But I was worried about what my parents would say.

Mom was away that day doing some kind of special workshop. But my dad was there on the front steps waiting. The school had called him at his office. As soon as they told him what had happened, he knew where I was heading.

Dad didn't say a word to me. He just opened his arms and I fell into them and started to cry. After I'd gotten through crying, he took me inside and had me drink a glass of water. Then he drove me back to school. He didn't come in with me. I knew why that was without his having to tell me. I had to take responsibility for what I'd done. All he said, before giving me one more big hug and a kiss on my sweaty cheek, was one sentence that I've never forgotten.

"*Nittaunis,* my daughter, just remember that no matter how fast you run, you can't run away from your problems." He must have gotten that from Grama Delia.

After the accident it was all too much for me to bear, losing my mom and dad like that. Lots of days I wished I had been killed too, that the rest of me was as numb and unfeeling as my hand. Then I started to run again. It took me a little bit to get my balance right. My body was stiff, and my left hand threw me off at first. It all came back, though, and I was as fast as I'd ever been. Maybe even faster, because my legs had gotten longer and my stride was just as swift. And running made me feel alive

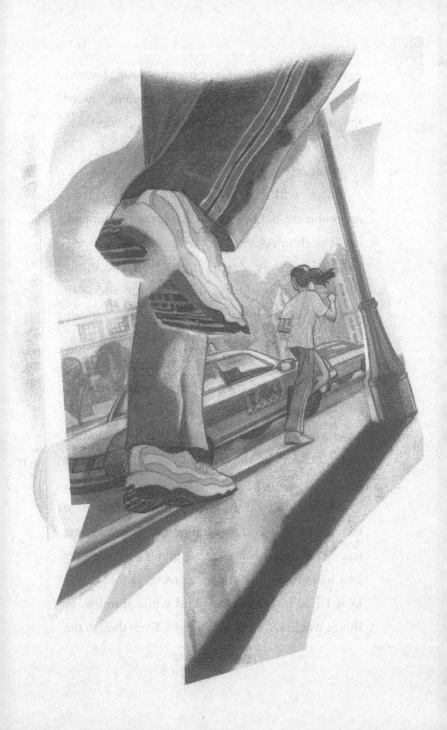

again. No matter how far or how fast I ran, I wasn't running away from anything. I was running toward the memory of my parents' loving arms, always there to catch me at the end. Running.

Running.

Roger and I were running hard. Not away from my problems, but toward them. Our arms pumped, our legs churned, our breath was even and strong. I don't know how much adrenaline I had in my system, but it seemed as if I could run and keep running forever. Even though I knew deep inside me that it wasn't solving anything, I felt as if I was in control of things while I was running.

A horn sounded from the street next to us.

"Maddy," Roger said, "Maddy, come on." Roger was turning toward the sound of that horn, slowing down, heading for the taxi that was pulling up next to us.

My feet didn't want to stop, but I forced them to. Part of my mind was telling me to keep going too. We'd only been running about five minutes and hadn't reached our rendezvous point. It was as if I had to get to that point while running, or things would not turn out all right. Even though the logical part of me knew that the sooner we got into a car the better, I went through a mental wrestling match, convincing myself to do what I knew was best.

"Madeline, come, come, come," said the taxi driver, holding the door open for me.

Of course, the driver was Mr. Patel. As soon as Mrs. Jenkins got him on the radio, he had figured out what our route would be to the pick-up point and reached us well before we got there.

I should have felt relieved. But now that I'd stopped running, every feeling of calm or relief left me. My legs were shaking as I got into the cab, and all I could think was that no matter how soon we got home, it would be too late.

20

THE OPEN DOOR

MR. PATEL DID what any responsible adult would have done from the start. As soon as we explained to him why we were so upset and in such a hurry to get home, he called the police on his radio.

"This is R. G. Patel. I am the owner of the Providence Taxi Company. I am calling to report a probable home invasion. I believe it is connected with the recent animal mutilations. You must send assistance immediately. Yes, yes. Here is the information."

Then he read off the number of his license and gave the police the address of Aunt Lyssa's house.

Mr. Patel hung the microphone back on its hook.

"It is good," he said. "With any luck, the police will be there soon after we reach the house. It may be that just seeing our cab pull up to the door will frighten away this intruder. Such men are usually cowards."

Such men. Of course, we hadn't told Mr. Patel what we were really afraid of. Not a person, but a bloodthirsty monster out of a Narragansett legend. We'd just told him that we thought the person who had killed those animals was in my house, and had lured my aunt home by calling the library and saying I'd been hurt.

"He probably said that he was a policeman or something," I had said, "and that I was at home waiting for her."

That was all it had taken to convince Mr. Patel that a call to the authorities was of the utmost importance. It had also convinced him to break every speed limit in Providence. Even though he still diligently used his turn signals, he made each of the corners on two squealing tires, and the powerful engine of his taxi roared as he pressed the accelerator to the floor each time there was a straightaway. He even went around the barriers across the road at the construction site. The workmen had gone home early for the day because of the bad weather. I remembered hearing a story about how no one ever uses dynamite on a day when lightning might strike and set off a catastrophic blast. There was a single strip of undamaged road left that we sped down, past the idle equipment, including a truck marked EXPLOSIVES parked to one side, well away from the place where they had been blasting.

A quick turn, properly signaled, and we were back on the main road again. Aunt Lyssa's house was only a little ways away now. Another taxi was coming down the street toward us. Had it just dropped my aunt at the house? I had my hand on the door handle. Roger was holding my other elbow, which was probably a good idea. I was so keyed up that I was ready to open the door and jump out, even though we were still a block away.

But as soon as we screeched to a stop, the most amazing thing happened. Mr. Patel threw the cab into park and turned it off in one motion, did what looked like a forward roll across the front seat, and went right through the passenger side window to land on his feet on the sidewalk outside the cab. As a result he was ahead of us, his arms outstretched to hold us back as Roger and I piled out of the cab.

"We should wait for the police," Mr. Patel said, keeping himself planted firmly in front of us.

"No," I said. "No!" I tried to push past Mr. Patel, and struggled to pull my elbow out of Roger's firm grasp.

He nodded his head, seeing how frantic I was.

"All right," he said. "But we shall go together, carefully."

We approached the front door. Part of my mind was registering things that were a surprise to me. Mr. Patel wasn't just a taxi driver. He owned the cab company. And he'd actually gotten out of his cab. Now that I saw him fully on his feet, I was amazed at how tall he was, almost big enough to be a basketball player.

But what pushed all of that into the back of my mind was what I saw as the three of us went up the steps. The front door was slightly ajar, as if someone in a big hurry had just gone inside. My aunt's key ring was hanging from the door, her key still in the lock.

"Aunt Lyssa," I yelled. "Aunt Lyssa, get out of there!"

21

SEARCHING

REMEMBER WHAT I said about the way Roger and I criticize the way people act in certain movies? You know, those scenes they seem to have in every single scary film. Like the one where the kids go right in through that open door, when you just know a monster is waiting for them. You know, just so the werewolf or vampire or brain-sucking mutant from outer space can pick them off at its leisure one by one. And everybody goes:

"Yeah."

"Great idea."

"Cool."

"Let's all wander off and get massacred."

Guess what we did as soon as the three of us saw that open door? Naturally we went right inside and split up, me still loudly calling my aunt's name.

A convenient way to let whatever was lying in wait know that its next dinner course had arrived.

"AUNT LYSSA!" I shouted.

There was no answer. I should add that in her old house, that isn't unusual. For someone to yell and no one to answer, I mean. The walls are thick, and the way the carpeted hallways turn corners seems to deaden the sound. You can't hear anyone calling to you even if they're only two rooms or a floor away. It's great to be able to play your music as loud as you want and know that no one is going to tell you to turn it down because no one can hear it except you. But it is not so great when you are trying to find someone. You'd be amazed at how often on a normal day Aunt Lyssa and I find our-selves playing involuntary hide-and-seek with each other as we go from room to room calling each other's names until we finally meet up more or less by accident.

So what did I do then when there was no answer? Of course, I acted out scary movie cliche number two. I ran upstairs on my own. My feet thumped on the stairs, their beat only a little louder and more frantic than my heart. As soon as I reached the top, I called my aunt's name again. There was still no answer. And unlike that famous scene in *Psycho*, no homicidal maniac with a big, long knife jumped out to stab me in the heart.

But as I started to approach the closed door to my aunt's room, a long-fingered hand suddenly grasped me hard by the elbow.

"Maddy, don't run off like that," Roger said.

Mr. Patel was close behind him. They had come up the stairs after me. The two of them apparently were unwilling to follow the "Let's split up and get gruesomely killed one at a time" scenario.

I took a deep breath. I needed to get a grip on myself and start acting like I still had some sense. I closed my eyes for a moment, listening for the memory of my dad's voice, thinking what he would say to me right now.

Be calm, Nittaunis. Maumaneeteantass. *Be of good courage.*

"You're right," I said.

"We will stay together now," Mr. Patel said, looking down over Roger's shoulder at me. "Yes?"

I nodded my agreement. Then, together, the three of us thoroughly checked out each of the five upstairs rooms. We looked behind the doors, in the closets, under the beds, and in the stand-up wardrobes. We even peered up at the ceilings, but all we saw hanging there were a few small spider-webs, no Dracula-fanged black-robed figures waiting to fall on us from above.

Together we went back down the stairs. There was still no sound of approaching police sirens. I looked at the hall clock. It seemed as if we had been looking for my aunt for hours, but our search had taken us no more than five minutes so far. We made a semicircle through the house, walking through the entranceway, the sitting room, the front dining room, the small back porch, the closet under the stairs. Just as before, we found nothing. No sign of Aunt Lyssa, not even her purse.

But there was one more place to look. The one place I had unconsciously saved until last because I didn't want it to be the place where we had to go. As we entered the kitchen, I opened the cupboard and pulled out the largest flashlight, an electric lantern that was as big as a club.

"Here," I said, handing it to Mr. Patel. Then I gave Roger the next-largest one. I didn't take a flashlight myself, even though there were two left. I guess it was a mistake on my part, considering what happened later. But if you had only one good hand like I do, you might have hesitated, too, about not keeping it free.

"There's one more place to look," I said.

Then I led them around the corner to the cellar door.

As soon as I looked at it, I felt my knees grow weak. It was unlocked.

22

THE CELLARWAY

THE HEAVY CELLAR door creaked on its ancient hinges as Mr. Patel pulled it open.

I've always been freaked out by cellars.

With all the reading and movie watching that Roger and I do, I know some of the theories about why this is. Roger's mom even incorporates it into some of her lectures, especially when she is talking about Providence's own first master of horror, Edgar Allan Poe. The "motif of premature burial" is how she puts it. When you descend into a cellar or a cave, you are "presaging your own interment," walking down into your own grave before you are dead. The worst thing Poe could think of happening to any of the characters in his stories was to be walled in or buried alive. Like that guy who is walled into his own wine cellar in "The Cask of

Amontillado" or Ligaea in her tomb. Poe was so scared of being buried alive himself that he even designed ways to put bells and speaking tubes into his own casket.

Back in Poe's time, they didn't embalm people, but just buried them really quick before they started to smell bad. Sometimes they did make mistakes and put people into the ground when they had just gone into a coma or something. Then they would wake up six feet underground in a coffin. That is also, according to Roger's mom and some of the stuff we've read, one of the sources of the whole vampire myth. People would dig up a coffin and find the dead body in it still sort of fresh, with blood on its hands and a contorted, scary face. But that dead person didn't look like that because he or she was a bloodsucking monster. It was just because that unlucky person had been buried alive, came to, and then tried to claw out before finally dying of hunger and thirst and suffocation.

I admit that being buried alive is grim. But premature burial is not one of my phobias. I'm just plain scared of what might be down there. It's not only H. P. Lovecraft who thought that underground tunnels were used by terrible creatures hungry for human flesh. Lots of our Indian legends, like the one about the Whisperer, tell about monsters using such tunnels, about caves where horrifying and evil creatures are kept locked away so they cannot harm the world.

"There's a light switch to the right just inside the door," I said to Mr. Patel.

My words came out as something between a croak and a whisper. I was so scared that I was trembling, and I was clutching Roger's hand just about hard enough to break his fingers.

Mr. Patel leaned forward, his fingertips brushing the rough wood of the stairwell wall. I tensed up, sure that at any second there would be a scream and then something—a bony hand, a bloody claw— would snatch him down into the darkness. Instead there came the satisfying sound of the switch being clicked and the sudden glow of light from the single forty-watt bulb at the bottom of the stairs. It was twenty steps away, but it looked as far off as the tape across the track at the end of a hundred-yard dash. And it was so dim. A bulb that small in a cellar makes more shadows than it does light.

Mr. Patel peered down into the semi-darkness.

"We should wait for the police," he said in a way that made his words half statement and half question.

Roger and I looked over his shoulder down to the bottom of the stairs.

"No," I said in an urgent voice, letting go of Roger's hand and reaching out to tug Mr. Patel's sleeve. "We have to go down now. Do you see it?"

There on the bottom step, lying half open on its side, was Aunt Lyssa's purse.

MUST HAVE slipped under Mr. Patel's outstretched arm, because I found myself sitting on the bottom step holding Aunt Lyssa's purse between my knees while I searched through its contents: her wallet, her clip-on library ID badge, her credit card holder, her brush, her makeup case, her notebook with three pens attached to it by a rubber band wrapped tightly around it. Everything was there except for the one thing I was looking for.

Roger was next to me, sweeping the strong beam of the flashlight into every dark corner of the cellar, behind the furnace, up to the rafters. His light seemed as reluctant to penetrate the dark corners of the cellar as I was.

"It's not here," I whispered.

"What's not there?" he whispered back.

Whispered. A dark old cellar can have that effect on you, lowering your voice to a whisper and your anxiety to the brink of a scream.

"Maddy." Mr. Patel's voice was not a whisper, but it was much softer and more concentrated than I had ever heard it sound before.

"What?" I answered.

"These doors," he said, playing his torch beam over the three oak doors set into the stone walls. "They are going where?"

He walked over to the door to the right, looked back at me, and grasped the handle.

"Root cellar," I whispered.

Mr. Patel pulled the door open and shone the flashlight inside. Nothing. It was empty as the Count of Monte Cristo's cell after he tunneled his way out.

Mr. Patel stepped back and moved to the second door.

"And this?"

"Where they used to store the coal." My voice was getting softer now. I wanted to turn and run away, run back up the stairs to safety, even though another voice was screaming in my head that we

had to move forward, that we had to find Aunt Lyssa before it was too late.

Mr. Patel swung back the door to the coal storage room. Aside from the fossil glitter of a few chunks of coal, the beam of his light disclosed nothing more than the dusty walls and floor.

There was only one door left. The one I'd been dreading.

"It's locked," I said, my whisper so small and hoarse that I must have sounded like a baby raven. "We don't even have a key for it."

Mr. Patel's long fingers wrapped around the handle as his thumb pressed the latch. With a rusty click, the latch moved down. The ancient hinges creaked loudly as Mr. Patel began to pull open that final, unlocked door.

24

THE OTHER SIDE

KUPHASH.

That is the Narragansett word to tell some-one to shut the door. It was the one word that drowned out all the others echoing in my head. *Kuphash*. Shut the door. Shut it before we see what is waiting for us on the other side.

I thought I had been tense before, but now my whole body was like a violin string overtightened to the point where it is about to snap. I was sure that as soon as that door opened something would leap out at us. Mr. Patel may have thought the same thing because he held that heavy flashlight like a club, ready to strike a blow with it. Roger was attempting to position himself in front of me, trying to protect me from who knows what—while my old stubbornness, despite my fear, was reasserting itself as I tried to push him out of my way.

"Move," I hissed.

"Wait," Roger whispered back, still trying to play the part of a defensive wall.

"Be quiet."

Mr. Patel's voice was so calm, yet so urgent that Roger and I both stopped. The strong beam of Mr. Patel's flashlight revealed a narrow, low-ceilinged, dirt-floored passageway, slanting down, carved out of the living stone. We saw no dark, cloaked figure waiting to leap out at us. But we did see marks on the floor—what appeared to be the heel marks of someone being dragged backward. Those drag marks were clearly visible until the passageway turned suddenly to the side some fifty feet ahead.

"Listen."

Roger and I listened. We heard a faint sound, a scraping noise. And as the three of us stood there, we also heard something else from behind us and up the stairs, where we had left open the front and cellar doors. Was it the faint sound of sirens coming down the street toward Aunt Lyssa's house?

"Maddy," Mr. Patel said, "you must go upstairs

and tell the police we are down here. Take your friend with you."

"You're going down there after her, aren't you?" I said.

"If I do not do so, it may be too late, you see," Mr. Patel said.

"I see," I said back in my most stubborn voice. "And I'm going with you."

"Me too," Roger said. I felt like either hitting him or hugging him when he said it.

Mr. Patel could see there was no way to argue with us now. "Just stay behind me," he said, moving down the tunnel.

It was hardly necessary for him to say that. The passage was too narrow for us to get past him. Roger and I followed, moving sort of sideways so that we were next to each other, Mr. Patel's broad back cutting off all but the faintest glimmer of light from the big flashlight that he held in front of himself. For a while the light from the cellar bulb cast a faint gleam down the passage behind us, then we went around the corner and all that was behind us was darkness.

We kept going, staying as close together as

possible. Whenever I glanced back, all I could see was the ancient night of the underground earth. What if we had gone past a secret opening in the wall? What if something was following us now? I wished I had brought another flashlight so that I could see, even though I was afraid that shining a light back behind us might show that we were, indeed, being followed by a legion of horrors. An active imagination is not your best friend when you are making your way through an ancient tunnel in the earth that smells of mold and moist decay.

If this tunnel had been used by the Underground Railroad, then it must have scared the life out of the slaves who were taken through it. They must have truly been desperate for freedom to go down into the earth like this almost two centuries ago, their way lit not by a powerful flashlight, but by the light of candles or pine-knot torches. Two centuries ago? This tunnel felt much older than that. Too much older. I found myself wondering just how long ago it had been carved through the stone and who had really made it. And when my ready imagination suggested an answer, I shivered and tried not to think of it.

Suddenly the tunnel widened. The three of us found ourselves standing side by side. The roof of the passageway rose above us, and there was the echoing feel of dark space around us. There were age-blackened, thick wooden beams here, used to prop up the high ceiling. I touched one with my hand, feeling the rough wood, so far from the sun that once made it the strong, tall trunk of a tree. You could see why such beams were needed. This place seemed much more unstable than the rock-walled passageway we'd just emerged from. There were small piles of rubble here and there, some that seemed to have recently fallen from the roof. I wondered if we were under one of the roads that had been built long after this tunnel was gouged out. Was it the road vibrations from heavy trucks that had made those piles of stones fall? What was it like down here when the construction workers on that street near our house set off one of their blasts? Would these old beams succeed in holding this tunnel from collapse for another century? For another year? Another hour?

Mr. Patel held the light of his torch to the floor. "Look here," he said, leaning close.

The drag marks were gone, as if whoever had been dragged had either started to walk or been picked up. Something metal glittered on the floor over to the side. Neither Roger nor Mr. Patel saw it, but I bent down and grabbed it up, knowing what it was. It was the one thing that had been missing from the handbag. There was no doubt now. Aunt Lyssa had been brought this way.

"Mr. Patel," I whispered.

"Wait," he said, "I hear something."

He swung the torch in an upward arc, then angled it down. There, ten feet in front of us, the floor of the cave fell away into a pit. I couldn't tell how deep it was, but I didn't want to look. Mr. Patel lifted the light and moved it slowly to the left.

I'm here.

Did I hear those words spoken in a harsh whisper or just imagine them? The hair stood up on the back of my neck.

I'm here.

Have you ever walked into a dark room and suddenly felt the sticky strands of an unseen spider's web across your face? Well, that is just how those words, words that only I seemed able to hear, felt to me. I felt like a little fly, its futile wings becoming more entangled no matter how hard it struggles, waiting for a hungry predator's poison-dripping pincers to bite down and suck out its life.

"Mr. Patel," I said in my softest voice.

Mr. Patel didn't answer. His attention was riveted on his flashlight beam. It had picked out something in the softer earth farther along the cave floor. Something that looked like the indistinct tracks of large, shuffling feet.

"He's here," I said, turning to Roger and poking him with my elbow. "Roger, I know he's here."

I clutched the little cylinder I'd picked up so hard that I thought the metal would crush like a soda can.

Mr. Patel held up his left hand, still slowly moving the light of the flashlight farther along the wall. "Hush, hush," he said. "There."

The beam of light picked out the shape of something creeping across the floor. Then, as it moved farther into the light, that something became a human hand. The moving torch found an arm connected to that hand, a shoulder, and then the shape of a person crawling on the dirt floor of the cave, a person who made a soft moaning sound as she weakly tried to pull herself forward. My heart leaped in my chest.

"Aunt Lyssa!"

The three of us reached her at the same time. She was only half conscious. As Mr. Patel helped her sit up, Roger put down his own flashlight and pulled out his handkerchief to wipe the dirt from her face. I was so stiff with shock that all I could do was stare down at her.

"Aunt Lyssa," I said, "Aunt Lyssa."

I couldn't think of anything else to say, just those two words. I'd been so certain she was dead that it was just as much a surprise finding her alive. She opened her eyes and looked up at me.

"Madeline," she said weakly, a little smile coming over her face, her eyes squinting from the light of the torch. "Where am I?"

I didn't know how to answer her. It was as if I suddenly had too many words to say, but none of them seemed adequate. I mean, how do you tell a grown-up used to the common-sense, everyday world that they've just been knocked unconscious and then dragged underground by a midnight monster out of some Indian legend who wants to drink their niece's blood? I took a deep breath, knowing that I had to try.

But I never got the chance.

"Oh God!" Aunt Lyssa said, pushing herself back against the wall of the cave and pointing behind us. Her voice was hoarse with terror. "Oh my God! What's that?"

25

I AM HERE

THE THREE OF us turned as one. A shadow was lifting from the mouth of another tunnel leading off this main gallery. It rose higher and higher and seemed to be gathering darkness around it. Even the beam of Mr. Patel's light was absorbed by that cloak of darkness as the shadow gathered and deepened and loomed over us, its two red eyes glistening.

Strangely, even though my throat was too tight to shout or speak, I wasn't frozen by fear. I don't mean I wasn't afraid. It was just that the fear of what might happen had been more paralyzing than this moment when all my worst nightmares seemed about to come true. Perhaps it was because I heard my father's voice in my head. I heard it clearer than ever since the time of the accident.

Nittaunis, Maumaneeteantass. "My daughter, be of good courage."

"Maddy. Get back, honey!"

It was Aunt Lyssa. She was trying to get between me and whatever it was that was in front of us. She couldn't pull me back. I couldn't move. All I could do was stare at what was there before me. It was every bad dream I'd ever had turned real. It was as real as darkness itself, and I could feel its thirst for my blood. And there was no way to escape. The wall was to one side of us and that black hole in the floor, that pit, was right behind us now because we'd turned. We were truly trapped. But Aunt Lyssa didn't care about that. She didn't know it was the Whisperer in the Dark, a monster far stronger than all of us. But even if she had known, it wouldn't have mattered. Her own fear was far less than her desire to try to protect me.

But if she'd wanted to get in front of me, she would have had to wait in line. Roger and Mr. Patel were already there, both of them holding me back. As the four of us each foolishly tried to be the one most in danger from the awful creature that faced us, I found myself wanting to laugh and cry at the same time. And this small hope formed itself in my thoughts, that perhaps our courage and our mutual desire to protect one another was strong enough to defeat this monster.

But that thought died as quickly as a flame blown out by a cold gust of wind when the Whisperer spoke.

"Fooools."

Its voice was still a whisper, but so loud, so rasping that it hurt our ears as it filled the dark cave and echoed through its passages. I'll never forget that voice, its mocking, cold power, its absolute hatred for everything that life and love and light mean. All that and more was expressed in that one word it spoke, including a terrible hunger that could never be satisfied.

"You know who I am."

The Whisperer in the Dark spoke slowly, moving a little closer to us with each word, gliding as if it was flowing, not walking. Aside from those flame-red eyes, its face was still hidden, wrapped in its cowl of darkness, but I could imagine the ironic smile on its grim lips. It came to me then that the Whisperer in the Dark was playing with us the way a cat plays with a mouse. I'd once asked my mother why a cat does that, why it doesn't just eat its prey once it has been caught.

"It enjoys it too much to end it quickly," my mother said. "It likes the taste of fear."

Threatening us, tasting our fear, that was its desire almost as much as its intention to take our lives. It was playing, just as it had played with me since that first telephone call, using its power of fear to send its voice not just through the air but through the telephone lines. It could take us at any moment, but instead it held back, held back like a movie monster gloating over its victim. And perhaps that desire to deepen our fear was its weakness if it gave us time to think, to act in some way. But what way?

The darkness in front of us raised an arm. At the end of it, something glittered in the beam of Mr. Patel's flashlight—a handful of blades held above us like a scythe.

Suddenly Mr. Patel moved, more quickly than I have ever seen anyone move before.

"AH-YAH," he shouted, hurling himself at that shape, actually striking it and pushing it back. He raised the flashlight like a club to strike, but that iron-clawed fist swung back too fast, knocking the flashlight from his grasp to spin and land, still lit, still lighting our little scene of heroism and desperation.

The swirl of shadow and light was so sudden, so confusing, that it was hard to see clearly what happened next. But I saw more than I wanted to see. I saw Mr. Patel stagger back to the edge of the pit, trying to keep his balance. I saw the Whisperer in the Dark surge forward like a black tide. I saw that awful, clawed hand cut through the air with murderous intent. Mr. Patel's head disappeared from sight and he fell backward into the hole.

Roger stooped to pick up his own flashlight and shone it toward the pit.

"NO!" Aunt Lyssa screamed. But Mr. Patel was gone.

Roger swung the beam in the direction where the dark, cloaked shape had been. Nothing was there. He swung the flashlight beam back and forth wildly.

"Maddy," he said, in a choked voice. "Where's it gone?"

Suddenly something reached over my shoulder and knocked the flashlight from his hands.

"Madeline, child of Canonchet, I am here," a cold, inhuman voice whispered from behind me.

26

NEIMPAUG

I AM HERE.

It had spoken my name. It was the final time for me to hear those words. Its game was over. The Whisperer had come to claim my life. I turned around. Roger's flashlight had been knocked to the ground, but it still cast off enough light for me to see into the darkness that loomed over me. There was a face there. A pale, bitter face with deep, blood-red eyes, white eyebrows, a nose and cheeks as sharp as the knife blades that glittered from its hand. It was not an Indian face. No Narragansett ever had a face as devoid of humanity as that, even during those long-ago years when our warriors grimly sought revenge for the slaughter of our families. No. It was a face of darkness and steel and dry stone. There was no more emotion in that face

than there was in those knives held in its hand, razor-sharp blades whose tips were red with blood. Mr. Patel's blood.

All the fear I'd been feeling, even the smallest residue of it, left me in that moment. I felt a tingling at the base of my spine, the kind you feel sometimes when there is electricity in the air.

"Mauchag," I said, my voice as calm and steady as the beat of a drum. "No. *I* am here."

I felt the gaze of those dead eyes on my face as it paused, searching for some sign of fear and weakness. Just at that moment, Roger did the only thing he could think to do. Remembering what I had said to him about the Whisperer's hatred of bright light, Roger pulled out of his pocket the laser pointer I'd taken from Aunt Lyssa's desk and shot a sharp beam of red light directly into the creature's face.

"Arrrsssshh!"

With an angry hiss, the Whisperer lifted up its cloak to block that painful ray, whose brief touch seemed to have left a red welt on its cheek. Its attention was turned away just long enough for me to raise and aim the cylinder Aunt Lyssa had taken from her purse when she entered her house and sensed that something was wrong. She must have still had it clutched in her hand even after the Whisperer had knocked her unconscious, only dropping it as she was dragged along the tunnel. I pressed the button, emptying the entire can of pepper spray into that evil face.

"RAWRRURHHHH!" The Whisperer in the Dark rocked backward, grabbing at its face with its hands, including the hand that held those blades, blades that cut into its own face as it tried to wipe away the wet, biting pain of the spray.

"ARRRGGHH!" it roared, so loudly that the walls of the cave shook around us. Half blind, it blundered into one of the support beams, splintering it into dust with a great blow from its arm. It swung its steel-clawed hand back and forth wildly, cutting the air, seeking flesh to rend and tear as it continued to scream. It was a scream that seemed filled with more anger and frustration than pain.

It was then, just as before, that Narragansett words came to me. They came to me as that tingling spread from my spine to my fingertips, an electric charge that I felt in both my good hand

and my dead hand. I held both my hands up toward the sky that I knew was somewhere above our heads.

"*Neimpaug!*" I cried. "Thunder! *Anunema!* Help me!"

Then the whole world exploded.

27

EXPLANATIONS

ROGER REMEMBERS WHAT happened next better than I do because I was knocked unconscious. He remembers the roof of the cave falling in, tons of rock coming down right on top of the Whisperer in the Dark, but not a single stone striking him or me or Aunt Lyssa. He remembers looking up and seeing the light of the sky fifty feet above us. He remembers the three of them carrying me up out of that hole in the ground and emerging in the middle of the street that had been under construction two blocks away.

Yes, I said the three of them. Roger, Aunt Lyssa, and . . . Mr. Patel. The pit he had fallen into turned out to be only six feet deep, and the fall had done no more than stun him.

"It is thanks to my yoga training," he said, "that

I was able to fall just so."

That yoga training had also enabled him to bend the upper part of his body back so quickly when the Whisperer swung its deadly iron claws at his neck. He had been wounded, but the wounds were no more than four deep slashes across his upper chest.

Why had the street exploded above us? There was sort of an explanation for that. Even though no rain fell, a sudden bolt of lightning shot down from the sky and hit the explosives truck. What couldn't be fully explained was why it happened at just that moment. It was a freak accident of the sort that no one could have expected, any more than they could understand why the force of the blast had been directed straight down in such a way that it opened the roof of the hidden cavern.

There were a lot of things no one could fully explain that day.

The police, though, said they knew who the Whisperer in the Dark was. His name, they said, was Wilbur Whateley. He had been born an albino, his skin so devoid of pigment, his eyes so sensitive that bright light pained him, and he was raised in a home where there were suspicions of terrible abuse. That was probably why he had taken to killing and decapitating animals when he was a child. Wilbur also apparently loved knives. He'd been taken from his birth family and put into the foster care system. Thirty years ago, when he was only thirteen, but bigger and stronger than most grown men, he had murdered his foster parents in the middle of the night. Then he sought out his biological parents and grandparents. He found them, too. When the police caught Wilbur, he was walking down the road with a big bag over his back. I don't have to tell you what he had inside that bag.

His childhood home had been just two houses away from Aunt Lyssa's. That was probably why he had discovered the caves and knew them so well. And that was why he came back to this neighborhood after he escaped from a mental institution two weeks before he called me on the telephone. How did he know my name and that I was a descendant of Canonchet? He had probably gotten that from reading the article about my winning the interstate cross-country meet.

"Wilbur Whateley," Roger said, shaking his head.

"I know."

It was too weird. Wilbur Whateley was the name of a character in HPL's "The Dunwich Horror," a bent, goatish giant who was half human and half the spawn of a creature from the depths of horror.

Whether he was actually the Whisperer or Wilbur Whateley, no one was ever able to prove. His body was never found in the massive cave-in, which also seemed to have collapsed the whole network of tunnels leading to that cavern.

When I told Grama Delia the whole story, her response would have been surprising to some.

"*Chauquaco Wunnicheke*," she said, nodding her head. "Knife Hand. Those dang diggers let his spirit out." Then she smiled at me. "I am proud of you, grandchild. You have your father's courage."

Following Grama Delia's lead, the Narragansett Tribal Council got the town to close down the excavations of that cave and to put back everything where they had found it, even though rumor had it that they'd already uncovered some very interesting items. Did those things include the skeleton of a huge man and a rusty five-bladed knife? I really can't say. But I can tell you that Grama Delia and several other elders who remember our medicine supervised the blocking of that cave mouth, not just with stones, but with reinforced concrete and a layer of earth over that. Then they did a certain ceremony. Grama Delia made sure I was there to see it, but I can't say anything more than that, aside from the fact that Mr. Patel and Roger and Aunt Lyssa were the only non-Narragansetts present.

My life is back to normal now. As normal as my life can ever be. Like Bootsie, who is back to running around like crazy in our backyard after imaginary squirrels, any scars I may have aren't visible. I'm still reading horror stories and going to monster movies and talking about it all with Roger. I've even begun thinking seriously about writing stories like that myself. Roger has been encouraging me. That's the main reason I wrote down my recent experiences. His mother encouraged me to do it too.

"Turning a traumatic experience into fiction," she said, "is a wonderful technique for giving you power over it."

Last night, when I read the last chapter to Roger, he said it was great. Then he put both arms around me and hugged me. I hugged him right back. I used both arms, because even though my left hand is still not as sensitive as my right hand, I've been able to move it a little and I can feel hot and cold with it now. It's been that way ever since the explosion in the cave.

Roger smiled down at me and then he kissed me. That was a first. And, as far as I am concerned, a fine way to end my own scary story.

MICHAEL GREENLAR

JOSEPH BRUCHAC is the author of SKELETON MAN, THE RETURN OF SKELETON MAN, THE DARK POND, NIGHT WINGS, and BEARWALKER, as well as many other critically acclaimed novels, poems, and stories, many drawing on his Abenaki heritage. Mr. Bruchac and his wife, Carol, live in upstate New York, in the same house where he was raised by his grandparents. You can visit him online at www.josephbruchac.com.

For exclusive information on your favorite authors and artists, visit www.authortracker.com.

9 780060 580896